The Dysfunctional Affair

Hadena James

All rights reserved. Except as permitted under the U.S. Copyright Act of 1976, no part of this publication may be reproduced, distributed, or transmitted in any form or by any means, or stored in a database or retrieval system, without prior written permission of the author.

This book is a work of fiction. Any names, places, characters, and incidents are a product of the author's imagination and are purely fictitious. Any resemblances to any persons, living or dead, are completely coincidental.

Copyright © Hadena James 2013
All Rights Reserved
ISBN: 978-1490543314

Acknowledgments

Thanks to Jason and Mollie for letting me work.

Huge thanks to Eliza Bay, my content editor and Krissy Smith, the proof reader for their work on this book.

Also By Hadena James

Dreams & Reality Novels
Tortured Dreams
Elysium Dreams
Mercurial Dreams
Explosive Dreams
Cannibal Dreams
Butchered Dreams
Summoned Dreams
Battered Dreams
Belladonna Dreams

The Brenna Strachan Series
Dark Cotillion
Dark Illumination
Dark Resurrections
Dark Legacies

The Dysfunctional Chronicles
The Dysfunctional Affair
The Dysfunctional Valentine
The Dysfunctional Honeymoon
The Dysfunctional Proposal
The Dysfunctional Holiday

Short Story Collection
Tales to Read Before the End of the World

Prologue

My life is a disaster of my own making. Well, that isn't entirely true, I have help from time to time in the disaster area. For example, on any given day, it is possible that a particular someone will try to run me down with a car. It is also possible that the Russian mob will show up at my door. Or worse, that my mother and her sisters will show up at my door.

Vacation Blues

My cell phone rang. I checked the flashing caller ID and grudgingly hit the talk button.

"This is Nadine," I said quietly.

"How was Russia?" Zeke Laroche asked.

"Beautiful, magnificent, breath-taking, amazing," I paused, "if you give me a second I can probably come up with some more adjectives, but they won't do it justice."

"I get the picture. I need to talk to you."

"Uh, today's not good; I have tons of things to do." This was the truth; I'd been in the office three days, and hadn't gotten anything done. Even my email had been left unread. I knew I had a case of the vacation blues, but wasn't sure what to do about it. I'd bawled on the return flight, hating the idea of leaving Russia.

"I'm sure you do." The door to my office opened. Zeke stepped inside, squeezing the phone closed. "But Lucy says you haven't sent her a single email all week, so you obviously aren't looking at them."

He checked the ceiling before taking a seat across from my desk. This had become standard operating procedure since a pencil fell down, hitting Anthony in the head.

"What's up?" I sighed, resigning myself to the task of talking.

"You haven't read your email."

"Sure I have."

"Liar, if you'd read it, you'd know I was currently homeless."

"Oh, yeah, about that," I groped for something to say. I hadn't read a single piece of email and had no idea what he was talking about. "I'm sorry about the fire; did you manage to save anything?"

"What?" Zeke shook his head and closed his eyes, a smile curling up the corners of his mouth. "My house didn't burn down."

"Oh, was it flooded?" I folded my hands on the desk. Zeke shook his head again. "Infested by termites, rats, maggots, in-laws, ghosts, poltergeists, zombies?" He shook his head at each of these suggestions, the smile wider as my suggestions became more ridiculous.

"You aren't even close."

"All right, why are you homeless?"

"Denise tossed me out about six months ago. I've been living in an apartment, but the neighbors are complaining about the hours I keep. I need a place to stay for a while."

"Did you ask Sebastian?"

"Yes, he's sleeping on Jacob's couch. His girlfriend tossed him out too."

"Oh, well, what can I do?"

"You have three extra bedrooms. I could rent one from you for a while."

"Me?" I frowned harder. "I don't think that's a good idea, I mean I am your boss."

"Nobody cares; several suggested I contact you about a room."

"Why?" I couldn't hide the surprise.

"I can't tell you." Zeke smiled.

"Well, who said it?"

"Again I can't tell you that. If I tell you, you'll get pissed off and spend the next three weeks bitching at everyone and giving them shitty assignments."

"Oh, come on, you're killing me. I have to know what they said. I promise not to get mad. If you don't tell me, it's going to drive me crazy." I have enough curiosity to kill at least fifteen cats. I really hate it when people allude to things, and then don't tell me what it is."

"Well, if you sign a contract about leasing me a room for six months, I could probably tell you what they said. But, you have to sign the contract first."

"That's blackmail." I pushed the intercom button.

Lucy appeared with a small stack of papers. She set them down on the desk, directly in front of me.

"We typed the contract last week," Lucy pointed where I was supposed to sign.

"Fine." I quickly glanced at it, signed where indicated and passed it to Zeke. He also signed. "Now you have to tell me who said what."

Lucy raised an eyebrow. "I said that you needed a roommate and babysitter and that if Zeke wanted to stay with you, he'd have to blackmail you into signing the papers. Then during last week's staff meeting, a couple of people said, 'stay with Nadine, she has tons of room.'" She smiled as she exited the room.

Zeke stood up. "Sorry, Nadine, but it's been a bad week. I had to do something."

He also left. I sat there, pissed that I'd been tricked by the two of them. I tossed a pencil at the ceiling and watched as the eraser hit the tile and fell back down. It landed, lead first, on a stack of folders. The top folder was marked "if you don't read these soon, I'm going to superglue them to the windows of the Hummer." I grabbed the folder, pretty sure that Lucy was serious about the superglue. That would be impossible to clean up.

Right on top of the stack was an agenda for a staff meeting. I looked over it. It didn't sound all that important. I pushed the intercom button again.

Lucy immediately returned to the room, carrying a clipboard, taking the seat that Zeke had vacated. Her face was pleasant and she seemed amused. She noticed the folder in my hands.

"No, you may not reschedule the staff meeting," she said taking a seat.

I shook my head, "Why not?"

"Do you have any idea how hard it is to get a time when at least fifteen people can attend a meeting? There are some scheduling conflicts that need to be ironed out, some general grievances about current working accommodations, ideas for the next office party, ideas for the summer picnic, the current lawsuit, the publicity we've been receiving, the stepping up of our own security until the publicity goes away, ideas about a press release in an attempt to divert attention from our work and your lieutenants would like a follow up staff meeting regarding safety and your ideas on what to do for the people you've helped. I think that about covers it."

I scanned the agenda and saw none of those items. "Did we print a fake agenda?" I asked suspiciously.

"Yes, there was a disagreement about whether you would try to take the day off if you found out what was going to be discussed."

I nodded my head; it was a pretty slick trick. I would have to remember it.

"Huh, well, I'm working at getting over my vacation blues. I have every intention of being there."

Lucy smiled, "So you can't think of an excuse to run away."

"Nope, not a one," I smiled back at her. I crumbled the agenda and threw it in the general direction of my recycle bin.

The staff meeting was regarding a woman named Amanda Reed. A year earlier, Alex Zeitzev and I had helped her disappear. She was in an abusive relationship. What we hadn't known at the time was that she had stolen money before we picked her up. At the moment, we didn't know where the threats were coming from nor how much had been stolen. We also couldn't figure out how they knew Alex and I were involved. Now, we were getting death threats. It was part of the reason for my vacation to Russia. My family had connections there, connections that others steered clear of. It had been the safest place for me to be.

I made it through the staff meeting, but was very tired afterwards. Staff meetings were rough. When everyone is an alpha, there's a lot of talking over each other. I leaned back in my chair and felt my eyelids droop. I hoped a pencil didn't fall on my head while I napped

My nerves suddenly awoke with a panic that comes from being seriously startled. Adrenaline surged through body; my ears seemed to pick up every sound. It was the sound of light footsteps that had put me into hyper alert mode. I stood up from my chair and drew my gun, footsteps that light and slow were probably a bad thing. If it turned out to be nothing, I'd apologize later.

The doorknob gave a slight rattle as the door eased from the frame. Zeke walked in with a slightly amused look on his face. He looked down at the gun and then back to me.

"You really gonna shoot me?" He asked, closing the door.

"What the hell are you doing sneaking around the office?" I tried not to yell. The adrenaline was starting to slow down; I felt stupid. He took the chair across from me and I holstered the Berretta.

"You were snoring, I was trying to wake you without scaring you," he grinned.

I thought about it for a moment and checked my clock. Yep, I had definitely fallen asleep at some point. I fell back into my chair and was forced to compensate for its attempts to roll away. I rubbed my face and looked at the desk.

Zeke looked at me, "you still haven't read your email. My car is broken down." He said this slowly as if it was supposed to ring some bells. When I stared at him blankly, he continued. "Sebastian gave me a ride here, he's already left. Since I now live at your house, either you have to drive me home or give me the keys to the Hummer, because I'm not sleeping here tonight."

I stuck out my tongue at him. It wasn't entirely satisfying, so I blew a raspberry, as well.

Zeke laughed and stood up, walking out of the office. I debated staying an hour or so longer and decided I would probably get a more restful sleep at my house. I followed him out, turning off the lights as I went.

Danes and a Roommate

There are six dogs in my house, six large dogs. Great Danes are wonderful pets; they are affectionate, loving, protective, and loyal. There is really only one problem with them, they are inside dogs. Now a small dog makes a great indoor dog. However, a dog that stands over 36 inches from the floor is not the ideal candidate for the house. I have no idea why they were bred to be inside dogs, but they were. I absently petted the one closest to me. They would stay like this until I got up or until something caught their attention and they had to investigate. I figured as soon as Zeke started down the stairs, they'd be out of the room like lightning. This was one of the advantages of a big dog, if they were smart, they could figure out how to open doors. Especially since I had put in handle door knobs instead of round ones. I only had two that had learned how, but those two were able to let the others out.

The shower turned off and the dogs lifted their heads from the bed, listening to Zeke as he moved around in the bathroom. I waited quietly; the mad dash would begin any moment. They would fly off the bed, Loki or Set would open the door and then they'd scramble down the stairs. At least one would trip and slide to the bottom. I would wait until they were completely downstairs before attempting to get up and moving. It was much less dangerous.

I heard the bathroom door open and close, then the spare room door closed. Instantly, the dogs were off the bed and running for the door. By the time all six were assembled, Loki had gone to work. The door latch clicked, then it was pushed open as the dogs headed out. I heard their paws thud against the floor as they ran for the stairs. It was the sound of distant thunder, one that I was used to hearing. The boom intensified as they reached the stairs, still running at full speed. Then the yelp as one lost its footing and went crashing to the bottom. So far, only Set had suffered an injury from this falling spectacle. Then I heard Zeke yell as they crashed into him, happy and excited at the prospect of getting his attention. I stood up and dressed. Unlike the Danes, I calmly walked down the stairs.

"Holy crap," Zeke gave a small shriek. He grabbed the nearest dog, Enki, trying to hide behind him. I stared at him for a moment. Anubis and Loki were playing tug of war with a towel.

"Are you naked?" I asked.

"I had a towel," he looked at the dogs. "I usually shower, get a cup of coffee and then get dressed."

"How'd that work for you?" I asked, walking over to my biggest Dane and grabbed the towel from Anubis. It was covered in dog slobber. "You'll probably need another shower if you use this." I handed it to him over the back of Enki.

"Wow, that's nasty," Zeke looked torn between wrapping up in it or wrapping up with Enki.

I turned my back, trying not to laugh. I heard his feet move up the stairs. The dogs moved with him. He shouted at them to let go of his towel three more times as I sat down at the kitchen bar counter. A minute or so later, the group came back down the stairs. Zeke landed at the bottom first, splayed out like a murder victim. Marduk landed on top of him, his breath wheezed out dramatically. Suddenly the others were there too. They all piled on, licking and sniffing my new roommate.

I smiled at Zeke as he tried to pull himself from the mob. For my five foot two inch frame, the struggle was a long grueling battle that took ages. Zeke was not faring any better. I walked into the kitchen and got down a bowl. I was a cereal kind of gal. I had eight different kinds, I had very little of anything else in the cupboards. I poured some Crispix and added milk. I topped it off with a nice glass of OJ. I knew how to make a wonderful breakfast; juice and cereal was perfect. As I sat down, Zeke joined me at the table.

He looked at me and I smiled back at him. His face was red from the drool bath he'd just received. He grabbed a handful of napkins and started wiping his face. "Did you start coffee?" He asked sounding grumpy.

I raised an eyebrow at this. I am not a coffee drinker. I got all my caffeine from soda. "Uh, no, why would I?" I replied, trying not to look befuddled.

"Huh," he got up and walked into my kitchen. I ate my cereal quietly, smiling from ear to ear. It was nice to see someone else get attacked in the morning. If they exerted their energy on him every morning, I could get used to the roommate thing. He sat back down at the table. "You have no food."

I stared into my bowl. "Of course I have food. There is cereal in the cabinet by the stove, white milk, chocolate milk, orange juice, apple juice, Pepsi and left over Chinese in the refrigerator. If that's not food, I don't know what is." I thought about it for a moment, "There's also dog food in the garage."

Zeke glared at me, "I'm taking the morning off to go grocery shopping." He sounded irritated. "I have always heard you lived on take out, but I didn't believe it until now."

I laughed, "So what, you just thought every time you came to my house I was between shopping days?"

He looked at me seriously, "A lot of single people shop one day at a time, I figured you were one of those."

"I go shopping every time I run out of the essentials."

"What are essentials?" He asked, sounding doubtful.

"I've already told you," I retorted, "cereal, milk, soda, juice, and dog food. Did you wake up on the wrong side of the bed this morning?"

He made a disgusted noise and headed back to the kitchen. I was guessing Zeke was not a friendly person until he got coffee in him. As an after-thought I added, "I also keep coffee in the house at all times, just in case I have visitors."

"You give them coffee, but not food," he said from the kitchen. "That makes a lot of sense."

"I can order out for food; it is much harder to get good coffee from take out," I replied, not quite friendly.

"You're bizarre; you are probably the most bizarre person I know."

"Are you always this grumpy in the morning? Cause if you are, I'm going to crush your alarm clock that way I know I'm gone by the time you wake up."

He sat down, "Sorry, no I'm not always this grumpy in the morning. I'm just used to bacon, eggs, toast, bagels, etc. for breakfast. Cereal is not among my favorite foods."

"You're the bizarre one. There's an IHOP on the way to the office, call in an order and pick it up if you don't want cereal."

He nodded his head and looked at me, very seriously. I didn't like the look; it was the look people got when they wanted to talk to me.

Usually, it was not something I wanted to talk about. "Anthony is compiling a list of people that Amanda Reed might have stolen from. Most of them are dangerous."

I nodded my head. "It's probably a long list. He should also consider people that might just want to kill me and blame it on someone else. Criminals talk and while in Russia, the Russian Mob paid a visit to one of my cousin's because they had heard I was involved in something nefarious and they didn't want me bringing them a turf war."

"How many people are you talking about?" He took a sip of his coffee.

"I don't know really. But you have to admit, I'm a lot better at making enemies than friends."

"Seriously Nadine, can you think of a couple of people in particular that are pissed enough to want you dead?"

"How about the guy who occasionally tries to run over me?" For the last four years, I'd had to watch where I was when walking down the street because some jackass had a tendency to jump curbs trying to run over me. It only happened once or twice a year, but the police and Alex were at a loss to figure out who it was. The car was always stolen, and he rarely left evidence behind. In the beginning it had been scary, now it was just irritating. So far, he'd always missed because cars have to get some speed behind them to jump curbs and kill people, which means they make lots of noise. Plus, he didn't seem to want to hurt anyone else, he always chose a time when I was alone and not in a crowd. It gave me time to get out of the way. He'd only come close once, catching my thigh, tossing me back several feet, before he had to pull back off the curb to make his getaway.

"I'd forgotten about him." Zeke frowned, "anyone else?"

"I don't know. Occasionally I get threatening mail, but most of it is pretty lame. I mean, it's things like 'I'm gonna kill you, bitch.' Most people who threaten, don't follow through."

"Now you know the other reason we thought I should stay here. You are the most likely person to be a direct target."

"Oh goody," I let my spoon slide into my bowl. I was no longer hungry; I was angry and nervous. I actually hated trouble. It was a counterproductive hate. Without the threat of trouble, I'd be broke and out of business, but the idea of trouble made me kind of queasy. "Did he mention what I should be on the lookout for?"

"Since the money was probably illegally obtained in the first place, no. It isn't like they can walk into the office and start waving guns around demanding repayment," Zeke said.

I considered this prospect. I'm a paranoid alarmist, who does better when there is really a crisis. I don't make mountains out of mole hills and I don't run around screaming the sky is falling, but let someone shoot at me and I'm fine, let me think someone is going to shoot me and I go into panic mode. Life is funny that way.

Somehow, I made it into the office. I sat behind my desk, listening to music, trying to ignore the knot that had formed in my stomach. The knot was probably fear of dying, but Zeke was going to make me go shopping for cookware later; so there was another possibility about the source of the knot. Have I mentioned that I don't cook? I took Home Economics my freshmen year of high school and set the kitchens on fire trying to melt butter. Nope, kitchens and I didn't really get along.

There was a quick rap at the door. I stared at it, willing whoever it was to go away. This wouldn't actually work, but it was worth a shot. They rapped again, waited another second or two and then just opened the door.

Anthony checked the ceiling before coming too far into the room. When he'd decided it was safe, he took the seat across from me. He held a stack of papers in his hands. I was guessing those were the letters that might make the knot tighter.

"Are you busy?" He asked after a few more moments of quiet. The door hissed shut behind him, the latch clicking. No one ever shut my door; eventually, we'd put some kind of gizmo on it.

"Yes," I lied. "I'm willing you to go away."

"How's that working for you?" He smiled. It made him look younger, brighter.

"Not so well actually." I reclined in the chair, resigning myself to the task at hand.

"I've assigned Sebastian to do security for Alex, but she's throwing a fit."

Alex Zeitzev wasn't just my friend, she was a private detective, my cousin, and Russian. As such, she had more backbone than most and could be as stubborn as an alligator, possibly, just as lethal.

"Don't look at me, the women in my family terrify me. I'd rather deal with the Russian Mob than my mother."

Anthony nodded in understanding. We had a long history. He had once been hired by the Russian Mob to kill me. However, he found he didn't have the stomach to take out a ten year old girl. He became my protector instead. Now, he was my lieutenant, I did the paperwork and signed checks, because I had a business degree. He hired and fired staff and handed out assignments, because he was a hitman with a heart of gold. As a result, we had a thriving business.

"Amanda Reed isn't where you put her," Anthony said. "We've got people looking for her, but it appears she went to ground shortly after you dropped her off. Her new name and papers were never used."

"Who?"

"Kenzie." MacKenzie Reynolds was another friend of mine. She was also a cousin, on my father's side, and a private detective. It seemed to run in my family to either be cops or pretend to be cops. Of course, I never said that out loud to Kenzie or Alex, they would have both killed me.

Of course, I would have traded places with Kenzie at the moment. She got to look for bad guys, I got to go shopping and it wasn't for books, it was for household items. This was a complete waste of time and money. When Zeke moved, I wouldn't need anything except the microwave and the blender.

Shopping Woes

Shopping should be one of the circles of hell. It's tedious, time consuming and thoroughly aggravating. Zeke seemed to have an incredibly long shopping list that included everything from pans, to knives, to towels. I had two items on my list: a microwave and a blender.

At the moment, my microwave was working fine, but I had three dead ones in my utility room. Their deaths had been sudden and unexpected. My blender was on the fritz. It had dawned on me as we walked into the housewares department that should Zeke get the urge for a protein smoothie or a margarita, there'd be problems. First, he was likely to get electrocuted. Second, whatever he put into it was going to make it smoke. Finally, after a few moments of smoking, the base would kick the blender off of it and send ingredients all over my floor. I was certain the Danes did not need protein smoothies or margaritas. The three dead microwaves and dead blender had all died of the same cause: cosmic entertainment. I had terrible luck with gizmos and gadgets. Besides the microwaves and blender, I also owned a dead tablet, a dead ereader, two dead wireless routers, seven dead TVs, and a dead DVD player. People kept trying to get me to upgrade to a Blu-ray player, but it seemed like a waste of money especially since I didn't currently own a TV.

"Ceramic, Teflon, or glass?" Zeke asked.

"Ceramic and glass are the same thing," I said.

"No, they aren't. What would you prefer?"

"They're pans." I looked at the multitude of choices. There seemed to be hundreds. I guessed that if I got a set with lids, I could pop popcorn in them when Zeke moved out. "Well, some of them are pans. I don't think ceramic pans are a good idea. They'd break on me or on the Danes. I can just see one of them pulling a ceramic pan onto the floor and it shattering. We'll be picking shards of glass out of our feet for months. I guess as long as they aren't ceramic, it doesn't matter." I looked at the pans a moment longer. Zeke was reaching for a set of cast iron. "Wait, don't those have special cleaning instructions?"

"Yes, you have to wash them carefully and dry them a certain way," Zeke responded.

"And you think I'm going to do that? Plus, I don't see any lids. I need pans with lids."

"When you buy pans, you get lids. Have you never bought pans before?" Zeke frowned.

"Nope. I've bought a few pans individually, because my microwaves occasionally die, but I've never bought a set." I gazed at the collection again, found a set of blue pans and grabbed the box.

"Those are cheap pans, you don't want those," Zeke took them away from me and put them back. He grabbed a set of boring black and silver pans.

"Those are ugly," I commented.

"You don't cook," he replied.

"I might learn if I had attractive pans."

"No, you wouldn't."

"How do you know?"

"You've never bought an attractive pan."

"Good point." I shrugged.

"Knives next. Do you want ceramic or carbon steel?"

"They make ceramic knives? Wouldn't it break?"

"Ceramic and glass are not the same thing," Zeke sighed.

"Yes they are."

"No they aren't."

"Pretty sure they are."

"They aren't," Zeke glared at me. I raised an eyebrow, agreeing to disagree without saying a word. There was no way we were buying glass knives. I was unlucky. It would break and maim me, because the universe doesn't actually want me dead, just wounded. We picked out a set of carbon steel knives that said hand wash, which was good, because my dishwasher didn't work. I had loaded it one day, turned it on, and flooded my kitchen. I ended up throwing away all the dishes inside, because washing them seemed like a lot of work while standing in a puddle, waiting for the super cleaners to show up. I had them on speed dial. They gave me a discount.

We were discussing towels and why they had to be color coordinated when I saw her. The devil was walking towards me, in high heeled shoes that sounded like gunshots when they hit the floor. I scampered behind the towels, attempting to hide.

"Excuse me," the woman's voice made the blood in my veins turn to ice. "But I think my daughter was just standing here." She had seen me; I poked my head around the display.

"Hi mom, I didn't see you."

"Nadine, who's your friend?"

"Zeke. He is staying with me for a while." I replied, trying not to let my voice quiver. Did I mention the women in my family are terrifying?

"So, the two of you are shopping for household items?" She asked, looking in our cart.

"Well, sort of, I don't have stuff," I stammered. "It's hard to have a roommate when you don't have stuff."

"A roommate?" My mother seemed to think about this word for a minute. My mother was born in Russia. She'd earned her VISA by spying for the Americans during the Cold War. Once here, she'd married an Irish man and had five kids. I was the only girl and the middle child. She terrified all of us, even with most of her accent gone.

"I'm sorry, I didn't catch your name," Zeke held out his hand to my mother. In an instant, her face changed and she started smiling. Suddenly, I wanted to be as far away from the store as possible.

"Melina," my mother shook Zeke's hand. "Buy an extra microwave or two while you're here, it will save you a trip later." She whispered conspiratorially with Zeke, but not quite low enough that I couldn't hear her. Zeke's smile never faltered. "So, how did you two meet?"

"I work for Nadine, I'm only staying with her temporarily, since I'm divorced and trying to sort out my life."

"Divorced," my mother said this like it had meaning. She gave me a quick look that meant something, but I didn't know what. My urge to run was getting stronger. There was something going on, something I didn't understand, but knew was about to make my life more stressful. "Well, I'll let you two get back to it. I hope to see you again, soon." She emphasized the soon, and it dawned on me. I put my head against the display rack of towels. Zeke looked at me.

"Did I miss something?" He asked.

"My mother thinks we're a couple," I told him.

"A simple misunderstanding," he answered.

"You think that only because you don't know my mother," I told him. I didn't tell him that one of my brothers had gotten married because of a simple misunderstanding. Or that my other three brothers did not live in Kansas City or Missouri or Kansas because it made their lives easier.

~ 27 ~

"Are you going to cry?"

"Maybe," I answered. Actually, I would wait until she broke out the color wheel of bridesmaids' dresses before I started crying.

"Don't cry, I don't know what to do about crying."

"Stick around and my mom will make you cry too. Trust me, bigger men than you have fallen prey to her." I thought about Anthony. He understood. "When you have free time, talk to Anthony about Melina Daniels."

"Why do we need extra microwaves?" He changed the subject.

"They have a tendency to die around me for no reason. You should look in the utility room when we get back," I sighed. "It isn't a bad idea. I need a blender too."

"Interesting and unsettling," Zeke answered. I grabbed a stack of black towels. They wouldn't show blood like the others, I'd put them in the master bath. I shoved them in the cart. I had two more bathrooms. I grabbed a set of dark green towels because they looked masculine and shoved them in the cart. "Where are you putting those?" Zeke asked.

"The spare bathroom upstairs, which you will be using from now on. I don't know what sort of idiot built two entrances to the master bathroom, but it was obviously not a good idea," I scowled. In reality, I was the idiot that had asked for two entrances, just in case, I didn't want to be trapped and murdered in my own bathroom.

For the downstairs bathroom, I grabbed some bright purple ones. I had no idea what color the bathroom was, I wasn't that observant. However, I liked the look of them and they were just as soft and fluffy as the others. Besides, Alex's favorite color was purple, so she'd get a kick out of them.

"Where are those going?" Zeke asked.

"Downstairs," I answered.

"The downstairs bathroom is blue."

"How would you know?" I snipped at him.

"Because I've used it." Zeke replaced the purple with the blue. I replaced the blue with the purple. He grabbed the blue again. I took half the purple out of the cart and put them back. I grabbed half the blue stack from him and put them in the cart. See, I could compromise.

"Well, keep using it. If you use the one upstairs, it will probably just fuel the fantasies in my mother's head.

"Um, do you…" he started.

"Don't go there," I didn't look at him. "My mother has become involved. I must do everything possible to stop this freight train before it runs away."

"It can't be that bad."

"Oh yes, yes it can. My mother is a force of nature."

"So is mine, but she's still a wonderful mother." There was a tone to his sentence. I wanted to pry, but I didn't.

"Let's just get microwaves and get the hell out of here, before she comes back."

"We need more carts to get microwaves."

"Fine, you get the cart, I'll check out with these. Pick up a microwave and a blender." I told him.

"Okay," he gave me a strange look. I found the nearest register. The clerk told me the total and I stared at her for a moment. She said it again. "For towels and pans?" I asked, disbelieving. I could make a down payment on a car for that price.

"And the knives and sheets," she smiled at me. I swiped my debit card and shook my head. It was a small price to pay to help convince my mother that Zeke and I were not a couple.

Still shaking my head, I went outdoors and started packing the car. I was expecting my mother to show up and interrogate me about Zeke. I was in my thirties and unmarried. I might as well be an alien. Her goal in life was to see me married, which was why I had stopped dating. The last time I'd gone on a date, she had shown up at the restaurant and told him about how much money I made as an incentive for marriage. It had only been our second date. He had seemed interested, I had lost mine. The boyfriend before that had been subjected to her wedding planning skills after two months of dating. He had moved out of state when we broke up.

"Ms. Daniels?" A voice behind me said. I turned to answer and felt my body go rigid. Being stun gunned hurt like hell.

Kidnapped

"Ah, good you're awake." A voice floated to me through the dark. I struggled to open my eyes.

"Well, if that's what you want to call it." My voice was soft, my throat scratchy. I thought back to what had happened. I'd been packing stuff into my car and then, something. It was there, just around the edge of my memory. I tried to rub my eyes, but my arms wouldn't move.

"Ms. Daniels, I'm going to make myself very clear. You have information I want. Now we can do it the easy way, you answer my questions and I'll kill you quick or we can do it the hard way, I torture the information out of you." I still couldn't see the speaker, my eyelids felt glued to my cheeks.

"That's really lame. You should have rehearsed it before saying it." I muttered. My throat was starting to feel better. The heavy scratchy feeling was retreating. I really needed a drink. "May I have a drink of water?"

"Excuse me?"

"That's a really cheesy way to put it. You could have said something more original like 'tell me what I want to know or I'll slowly cut away chunks of your hair.' I don't know, just something more original." It was stupid to argue with him, but I couldn't really do anything else at the moment. "Water?"

"I don't think you are in a position to make jokes, Ms. Daniels." He was at least nice enough to put something to my lips. I drank it down. It was warm and definitely water. I hated water; it had a funny metallic taste to it.

"And haven't you ever heard torture isn't a very good way to get information." I continued after he'd pulled the glass away. "Under torture, you can get people to confess to just about anything; the information is usually whatever the torturer wants to hear. It's much more effective to schmooze a person, kiss a bit of behind, be their friend."

"Ms. Daniels, you are about to have the worst day of your life, maybe you should take it more seriously."

"Actually, the worst day of my life was June 20, 1999. I don't think torture and death can top even that day." I briefly wondered if I was dreaming as the words drifted from me. "See, that day, my first serious boyfriend dumped me, then I went to my best friend's house for comfort, but I was speeding and got pulled over. The ticket was almost $300! Anyway, I get there, she wasn't there, so I let myself in to wait for her, and some idiot neighbor thinks I broke in. The same officer that wrote the ticket, responded to the breaking and entering call. We had to track down my friend and wait for her to show up before someone would believe that I had permission to be there. We went out for lunch, because food is comforting, a little Italian place with some of the best ravioli in the world. I got food poisoning and now, I can't even smell pasta without feeling a little ill. On my way home, I pulled over to throw up and some idiot smashes into my car while I'm yakking in the grassy ditch. When I finally get home, my parents think I've been drinking and ground me for two weeks. Then as I'm walking up the stairs to my bedroom I lose my balance, fall all the way to the bottom, break my arm and dislocate my knee. If that wasn't bad enough already, it was my 18th birthday. I was leaving for college in two months, it should have been a really happy day, but no. Oh no, I can't have good birthdays. I haven't had a good..."

"Shut up! Do you always ramble when you're scared?"

"I'm not scared, I'm not even nervous at this point. I figure if you torture and kill me, my friends will have a nice big wake for me, and it still won't have been the worst day of my life. Besides, if you kill me I can come back and haunt you. That could be fun."

"My God!" He mumbled.

"What can I say, I'm an optimist." I tried to shrug and couldn't. "My dogs will probably miss me. But I can come visit them as a ghost."

"I'm going to duct tape your mouth until you start taking this seriously."

"Fine, but it will be hard for me to answer your questions if my mouth is duct taped. I could probably mumble through it, but it wouldn't be coherent. Once, when I was a kid, I started playing with my dad's handcuffs and cuffed my ankle to the water meter outside. It was raining, freezing cold, and there I was, unable to move. It took three hours before someone came to unlock me. I thought I was going to die of hypothermia and exposure."

"Your father is a cop?"

"No, he was a detective, until he died. He took a shotgun blast to the chest while in a gas station. He went in to buy a lottery ticket. Some junkie walked in to rob the place. When he saw my father's gun he just started shooting. Ironically, the ticket was a winner. My mom collected the life insurance, the winning lottery money, and his pension. What makes it even more ironic is that my mom was just about to leave him because he was a real jerk. Instead of a divorce, she got eighty-four million dollars. I thought it was a nice consolation prize for putting up with him all those years. She bought a new house, a new car, and retired. She's still living quite well off the proceeds of that. She even used part of it to put me through college. Some people are just lucky. Mom has always been that way."

"You're babbling again."

My eyelids finally loosened and opened. Not far, just far enough to see some light and shadows. Definitely an improvement over my previous state. Slowly, they adjusted to the light. I could see the man who had been talking. He stood about six feet from me, looking indecisive.

"Sorry, I just like to talk. My friends all complain that I either talk too much or not enough. I'm shy in big groups of people. I tend to sit like a fly on the wall, just listening. But one on one, I can hold up my end of any conversation and the other persons. I've...."

"Not another monologue."

"Oh, monologue, that's a big word. That's the other thing they complain about. No one actually talks like that. Well, no one but me. I'm always using big words that others have to look..."

"I am supposed to do the talking."

"That's another lame line," I muttered. "Fine with me. What would you like to talk about?" There was a method to my madness. A tracking device was hidden in my shoe. If I distracted him long enough, I wouldn't be tortured, and I really didn't want to be tortured. Plus, a person did have trouble torturing you, if they thought you were human.

He skulked over to me and pushed my head down. I stared at my knees and his shoes. My knees were kind of bloody, and I wondered if it was mine. I didn't feel hurt, but I was also pretty high on adrenaline.

"Your shoes aren't laced the same." I commented. Better to stare at his shoes than the blood.

"What?" The exasperation came through in his voice.

"Your shoes, they are laced different. It looks funny."

"Why does it matter how I lace my shoes?"

"Well, if you laced your shoes the exact same way it would show that you cared about your shoes. See, my shoes are laced exactly the same, left lace over right all the way up. They have the same length sti..."

"I'm beginning to think you're insane."

"That's technically a legal definition, not a mental health definition. I might have a personality disorder or two, but I am clearly not stark raving mad. I'm..."

"Shut up!" He hit me on the side of my head. For a few seconds, pretty lights exploded in my skull and it throbbed, then everything cleared again. "Jesus Christ, how did I get stuck with you?"

"Hey, you picked."

"It was rhetorical!" He sighed. "I want some information. Will you please give it to me without a fight?"

"I don't know, I keep trying to talk, but you keep interrupting me. How do you know I won't say something important if you never let me finish talking? I mean I don't know what information you want. How do you even know I have the info?"

"Shut up."

"How am I supposed to answer your questions if you keep telling me to shut up or you interrupt me? Is this the first time you've interrogated someone? If not, I think you're in the wrong line of business. I mean, if I was going to interrogate someone, this is not the way I'd go about it. Maybe you should go rehearse what you want ask. You don't seem to have your thoughts organized enough to do a proper interrogation."

He hit me again. It hurt, but then so did being tackled by six Great Danes and I survived that every day, a couple of punches to the face was easy.

"All right, Ms. Daniels, I'm going to ask you some questions. I want you to answer in short, brief statements, and you aren't going to deviate. If you deviate, I'm going to continue to hurt you. If I think you're lying, I'm going to hurt you. Do you understand?"

"Yes, but I make no promises to stay on topic. You seem to have a good vocabulary, which will help, because I won't have to stop and explain certain words. However, feel free to ask if I use one that you don't know. I don't want there to be a miscommunication because I overestimated your language skills."

"Do you know a woman named Amanda Reed?"

"Yes." I responded flatly. The cavalry was pretty slow today; I hoped they showed up soon.

"Did you help her disappear?"

"Yes." Yes, seemed to be a pretty good answer, he didn't hit me. Everyone liked hearing the word yes.

"Where did you send her?"

For a second, the wheels in my head turned, trying to find a city.

"Bogotá, Colombia." It popped out before I could stop it. Why I would relocate someone to the cocaine capital of the world was beyond even my imagination. It was obviously beyond my captor's too, he frowned at me. His eyebrows drawing together, his forehead wrinkling. He stared, puzzled for a moment.

"You sent her to Bogotá?"

"Yep." Might as well go with it now. Had I seen a movie or TV show about Bogotá recently? I couldn't remember, though it seemed unlikely since my TV was broken.

"Why Bogotá?"

"Would anyone ever think to look for her there?" Of course not, I wouldn't think to send anyone there either. "Kidnappings, drug lords, corrupt government officials, it's a writhing cesspool of crime. Why would someone look for a relocationee in Colombia? It probably has a higher crime rate than Miami and Detroit put together. And let me tell you." Pain exploded in my arm as he hit it with something. It didn't feel like a fist. "Hey, I'm answering your questions, you can stop doing that. Excuse me if sometimes I get a little side tracked; I have a lot of useless information floating around creating disorganized thoughts."

"Ms. Daniels, do you think this is some kind of joke?"

"Not really. I imagine you're pretty serious about your desire to find Amanda and kill me as necessary. That doesn't mean we have to be uncivilized about it. I'm telling you what I know, and you're just being an asshole. It makes me want to be less cooperative, especially since you've already told me I'm going to die."

"Fine, Ms. Daniels," he said through clenched teeth. "Why Bogotá?"

"I've already told you. Because no one would think to look for her there." I shook my head.

"I don't believe you."

"Why would I lie?" I met his gaze. He had very pretty brown eyes; it was too bad he was obviously a couple cards short of a full deck.

"All women lie, why do they do that?"

"I think it's too get more presents. See, if you lie..." Pain exploded in my thigh, this time I had seen the glint of metal. "Excuse me, are you stabbing me?"

"What?" The question seemed to take him off guard. I looked at the new spot of pain. Sure enough, it was starting to turn my blue jeans darker in that area.

"Did you just stab me? Well, imagine that. You aren't just an asshole, you're a bastard too. I'm wearing one of my favorite pairs of jeans and you are poking holes in them. I had considered being buried in them, but that's not going to happen now. Oh no, because you had to get knife happy. The blood can be cleaned up, but the holes cannot be repaired in time for my funeral. That just irritates the hell out of me."

"You're going to die anyway, why are you complaining?" He spat the words at me, forcing me to look up at him. Gazing at his face, I remembered it from a photo Alex had taken. The man ruining my clothes was Amanda Reed's husband.

"Because you could have at least left my favorite pair of jeans alone. I'm not walking around, stabbing holes in your favorite clothes, now am I? So I helped your wife hide. She probably ran away because you started making holes in her favorite clothes too. I have never." This time he didn't stab me, he just hit the area already wounded. It should have hurt like hell, but it was only a minor annoyance. I was running on pure adrenaline now; the pain would come when it stopped flowing, but not before then.

"Oh yeah, that's obviously working." I rolled my eyes, making sure he noticed.

"What are you mouthing about now?"

"Doesn't matter. I think you are the one who is clearly insane. I mean let's just take a moment to think about this. You've now stabbed me twice and punched me a couple of more times. All I'm really doing is bleeding onto the floor. It doesn't seem to be eliciting any useful information from me. I will eventually pass out from blood loss, and then you'll be right back at square one. Boy, you really are new at this. And what makes it worse is that you are clueless as to how ineffective it really is. Go ahead, stab me. You can stab me all day long, and it's not going to do a bit of good. I have had far worse injuries. Hell, someone once carved a word on my chest. I've been shot, beaten, stabbed, attacked by a tiger and hit by a car. That little bitty knife in my limbs is like getting a shot at the doctor's office."

"Shut up." He tossed the knife across the room. I was thankful it was gone, maybe I could survive now. "How the hell did you get attacked by a tiger?"

"Long story and I don't want to bore you with the details." I fought not to smile. His frustration was evident. While my situation still sucked, at least it was looking better. If I could just stay alive long enough, I would be saved.

"That would probably be the most interesting thing you've said all day." He sat back down, facing me. I would have preferred him up, pacing the room, clawing at the walls, but I'd take what I could get.

"Actually, it's not that interesting. I was attacked by a tiger. He got a good chunk of meat from my leg, I had physical therapy for two years and have a couple of really nasty scars, but, otherwise, it was just like any other day." Even the attack hadn't been that extraordinary. He was hungry, I looked like lunch. No harm, no foul. I never hold anything against large predators, they're just doing what instinct tells them.

"Fine, what would make you loosen your tongue?"

"I don't know, maybe if you knew one of my phobias and used that against me. Unfortunately, I'm not afraid of pain or death, so those are not effective. If you had asked me this earlier, we wouldn't have had to ruin my favorite pair of jeans."

"And I guess you're just going to tell me what you're afraid of?" He rubbed a hand down his face. It was a gesture I was used to, people did it to me all the time.

"No, but if you had done a little research before you kidnapped me, it would have helped. For example, my fears are pretty easy to discover. Just ask someone. Hell, even the press knows what I'm afraid of, I'm sure it's been printed someplace. And you would have known that I hire mercenaries, S.E.A.L.S and Rangers."

"What do your employees have to do with me?"

"Are you having a bad day or are you really this dense?" I shook my head. "They train for years on how to handle the stress of captivity and torture, not to mention how to deal with pain. You think I didn't pick up a few tips? Of course I did. My goodness, I wouldn't be very good at securely hiding people, if I didn't know how to handle pain. Otherwise, I'd crack the first time someone threatened to cause me pain. I mean, come on, you think you're the only person who has ever considered kidnapping me?"

"It's a miracle someone hasn't killed you before now. You are the most ridiculous person I have ever met." His eyes were wide and his face was a mixture of fear, hatred, frustration and disbelief.

"Well, it's not from lack of trying. I mean, I didn't shoot myself and I certainly didn't throw myself in front of the car. That really hurt."

"And the tiger?" He nearly groaned.

"That may have been my own fault." May have been was the understatement of the year. I spent three months working at a wildlife rescue center when I was in my teens, I would have stayed longer, but I antagonized the tiger. My boss really frowned on that.

"I should have kidnapped someone else."

"Probably."

"She's not in Bogotá."

"Nope, but you seem to prefer yes answers, and I don't remember where I moved her, so it worked." I tried to shrug and really couldn't. The knots binding my wrists were loosening though. If I worked a little harder, I could probably get free.

"You are..."

"Tedious?" I volunteered. Above me I heard a noise, instinct brought my head up to look at the ceiling. "Do you have pets?"

"No," he responded suspiciously. He looked up at the ceiling.

"Is your house haunted?"

"No," he was still trying to follow my gaze.

"Then I think you have mice." I looked back down at him.

"What?"

"I think you have mice. I can hear them moving above my head, sounds like they are in the ceiling. I bet I'm right under your kitchen."

"Do you have super hearing now?" He looked disdainful.

"No, I just hear really, really well." I heard the noise again, a slight shuffling sound. It sounded almost like someone dragging their feet gently across the floor. Maybe the cavalry had finally decided to put in an appearance. If it wasn't, I was going to bitch for weeks about how slow they were.

"I think you're trying to trick me into leaving the basement, leaving you alone for a while."

"Why do I need you to leave the basement?" I pulled my arms around in front of me, folding my hands neatly on my lap. "You tie terrible knots. I had it undone shortly after you stabbed my leg. Granted, getting you to leave the room would speed up getting my legs untied, but I don't necessarily need it. The knots work lose if you move against them. You should have taken a class in rope tying or you should have used duct tape. It's impossible to get out of duct tape without a knife and losing lots of skin."

He stared at me, mouth open. His gaze moved from my hands to my feet. He really was a crappy knot maker. The doorbell rang, making him jump. He looked at me, wiping the surprise off his face.

"Hmm, maybe it's not mice, maybe it was someone walking up the front walk that I heard." I frowned, milking the effect it had. "Usually, I'm better at pinpointing distance. Maybe the basement makes it sound weird. I can't believe you didn't hear it. Now, the moment of conflict. You have kidnapped someone and they are currently being held in your basement. Do you: A) leave them unattended while you answer the door, B) try to tie them back up and then answer the door, hoping the guest doesn't get suspicious about what took you so long, or C) stay in the basement and hope they go away."

"I'm not leaving." The doorbell rang again.

"Then let's hope it's the FedEx man, and not someone who knows you're home." I twirled my thumbs. "So, whatcha wanna do now?" I asked as it rang a third time.

"Fuck!"

"No, I'm not really up for that." I frowned.

"Shut up."

"Ok, I'm getting really tired of that. Would you please stop telling me to shut up?" There was the sound of breaking wood. The cavalry was finally here. Now, all I had to do was hope he didn't kill me before they got to the basement.

Luck was finally on my side. My captor jumped up and started towards the stairs, taking them two at a time. He cursed under his breath. I reached down and untied my feet, then just sat there. Above me I could hear people yelling for the suspect to get down on the ground.

"Nadine?" My brother, Ivan, shouted. He worked for the Kansas City police department as a homicide detective. This was just peachy. Rescued by my brother. All I needed was my mother picking out wedding dresses and it to be my birthday for this day to get worse.

Home Again, Home

Again

Zeke was snoring quietly in a chair when I opened my eyes. His head had dropped down, his chin nearly touching his chest. The room was mostly dark, the lights from outside filtered through the windows, giving it a strange glowing look. There was too much light pollution to show any stars, and I had a moment of sadness. I was obviously not at home. The sky at my house was only somewhat polluted, you could see the bright stars.

I listened to Zeke snore. I knew where I was and why I was there. Funny what the brain remembers even when it doesn't want to. The threat was obviously real now, the panic I'd been feeling earlier was quiet, leaving my mind available to think. My inane chatter had probably saved my life. He might not have been really sure about killing me, but the need to cover his tracks would have eventually won out over his desire not to kill. Knowing this calmed me even more. I would definitely have to take more caution next time. The clock on the wall said it was just after midnight, I hoped that meant it was Thursday. The Chiefs had the Thursday night game. Football would be good at removing the stupidity I felt about letting myself get kidnapped.

"You're awake." Zeke's voice was soft. I jumped at the sound. I had been lost in thought and hadn't realized he'd stopped snoring.

"So are you."

"Nadine, I'm sorry."

A nurse bustled into the room. She was about 5'4" tall with graying brown hair pulled tightly into a ponytail. Smile lines creased her face as she flipped on the light.

"So she is." She came in close to me. "How do you feel?"

"Not bad. Look, I want to get out of here as soon as possible."

"I think the doctors are going to release you late today or Monday."

"That doesn't exactly work for me." I smiled as she frowned at me. "See, the Chiefs play football in about twelve hours. That means in twelve hours I want to be at home, sitting on my couch, eating junk food and screaming at my TV." Her frown deepened. "Just bring in the waiver, let me sign it and I'll be on my way."

"Humph," she took my blood pressure.

"If it's not here in twenty minutes, I'll unhook my IV and walk out without signing the waiver." My smile widened. Zeke was hanging his head, trying not to laugh. A man wearing street clothes walked past the door. His face was lined and care worn, his hand clutched a cup of coffee in a death grip. I looked back at Zeke as a thought entered my head. "On second thought, I don't care who you have to wake up, I want that waiver now." I yanked the I.V. out of my arm, letting it fall to the floor.

The nurse let out a squeak as Zeke stood up. I swung my legs over the edge of the bed. The nurse nearly ran from the room as Zeke grabbed my shoulders.

"Nadine, what are you doing?"

"You can't protect me here, Zeke." I whispered, glancing back at the door.

"Check your hand."

I looked down and noticed a gold band on one of my fingers. I started to pull it off when Zeke grabbed my hand.

"They wouldn't let anyone stay, so I told them you were my wife. We didn't want you here alone."

"That's fine for tonight, but what happens at seven a.m. when they start letting in visitors? Anyone can just walk in here."

"They can't kidnap you from the hospital."

"No, they can't, but they sure as hell can walk in with a gun and silencer, and put a bullet in both our brains. Then they could just waltz back out the front door. How long do you think it would take someone to notice us? They'd think we were both asleep because the nurse is marking down in my chart what time I awoke." I shook my head. "This is an insecure location, Zeke, I have got to get out of here. What if that guy was just a warm up for the real thing?" I stole another glance at the door. "We can't talk here, but I want an escort out of this place. How long before a couple more people can get here?"

"We have three staying at Alex's, so maybe ten minutes. I'll make the call." He dug out his cell phone and talked into it quietly.

A doctor and the nurse returned. Both looked unhappy. I steeled myself to deal with them. Zeke walked into the hall.

"I think this is a bad idea Ms. Daniels." The doctor said as Zeke returned. His cell phone had disappeared again. "Mr. Laroche, please try to convince your wife she should stay at least until morning."

"You're married," Zeke pointed to the ring on the doctor's finger, "when was the last time you were able to convince your wife to do something she really didn't want to do?" It must have been a really long time or never, because the doctor sighed. "If she isn't in any real danger of dying, I think it's fine for her to leave. She has a phobia of hospitals, and it's not easy for her to stay." Zeke handed me a bag with my clothes in it. I felt sorry for the doctor and the nurse. I knew I was a difficult patient.

"Look, just let me sign the waiver, I'll call Monday and make a follow up appointment, but right now, I have to get out of here." I tugged on my jeans, noting that they were clean. Whoever brought my clothes had done a good job grabbing jeans, a shirt and socks, but had forgotten underwear. I could forgo them long enough to get home and behind a locked door. I wasn't panicky, but the hospital felt very insecure.

"There's no way I can convince you to stay until morning?" The doctor started talking again.

"Nope." I tore off the gown, yelping at the pain. Zeke rushed over and helped me into the shirt. I'd have to remember to move slower at home.

"Fine, I'll go get the instructions for your care." The doctor left the room. The nurse followed after making a few "humph" noises.

"Anthony is on his way to pick us up." He didn't meet my gaze.

"There's something you aren't telling me."

He sighed, "We've figured out where the stolen money came from. Fred Reed was laundering money for the mob."

"Russians?" I'd done that dance, and they hadn't attacked me in Russia, so it didn't seem likely.

"No, Italians." Zeke confirmed. "She stole a lot of it, over a million dollars. They've been letting Fred slide for the last year, but his time is up. The police have him in custody, but he's still in danger.

Kenzie has picked up a trail for Amanda though, she's following up."

"Mr. Laroche, here are the instructions for your wife's care. She'll need to have the bandages changed every six hours if she's bleeding or experiencing any drainage. If not, then twice a day should be enough. If the bleeding becomes excessive or if the drainage turns milky, yellow or green, she'll need to come back. I've written her a prescription for the pain. Try not to put too much weight on your leg." The nurse produced crutches. I stared at them. Crutches and I were not on very good terms. I'd sprained my ankle once and been put on crutches. The second day I used them, I fell off the porch and broke that leg. The break had needed pins to help it heal. I suppressed the urge to do a full body shudder. I signed the waiver as Zeke nodded that the Anthony had arrived.

Like all hospitals, they insisted on using a wheelchair to get me to the front door. Once there, I was on my own and I think the nurse was just fine with that. She handed me crutches that were going to be about as useful as a bag of soggy potato chips. Anthony gave the nurse his best smile as we exited. Ivan flashed his badge.

"Did you hotwire my car?" I asked Anthony, getting out of the wheelchair. I looked between him and the Hummer.

"No, Zeke gave me the key to bring him here when the cops called us." Anthony went and opened the door. I stood up on the crutches and took a step. It was only thirty steps, but it was going to be slow going.

"Give me the crutches," Ivan said, nearly yanking them from me. Anthony reached down: I skip stepped back from him. I wasn't entirely sure what he was about to do, but I was pretty sure it would make me feel feeble.

"My wife," Zeke hooked his thumb back at the door. Anthony turned, smiled and stepped away. "Relax Nadine." I wanted to see what they were talking about, but didn't have the balance to turn and look.

I let out a small yelp of surprise as Zeke picked me up and carried me the thirty feet to the Hummer. He put me in the backseat and slid in next to me. Anthony and Ivan took the front spots and we were off.

"What was that all about?" I asked as the tires droned on the road. The hospital disappeared behind us.

"The nurse was watching," Anthony didn't take his eyes off the road. "She scowled when I went to pick you up."

"Oh," I said, as if that explained everything. It didn't. I wanted to know why they hadn't let me walk to the car. Sure I was slow, but I doubted there were snipers stationed on top of the hospital. Even I wasn't that paranoid.

The Hummer slid into the garage. Anthony left the door open, Zeke stopped me from getting out of the car. None of us moved, as Anthony got out, leaving the Hummer idling.

"Stay here, we're going to sweep the house." Ivan and Anthony entered my house. The dogs were instantly excited, barking their heads off. I realized I was going to have to face the dogs. That was going to be a nightmare on crutches.

"Uh, can you guys restrain the dogs or let them outside when I enter the house?" I asked Zeke.

Zeke said nothing, he simply nodded and watched the opening where the garage door was. The Hummer still idled quietly. I wondered if Zeke would have time to jump into the front seat if something bad were to happen. However, I doubted someone was in there, not with the dogs.

Sure they were friendly, but they were also intimidating. They were an excellent deterrent. I turned to look out the back window too. My towels were still in the back, as were the pans, knives, a microwave, and a blender.

Anthony came back out of the house. Zeke leaned over the seats, turned the car off and opened his door. Anthony came over to my door, opened it, he helped me from the car, folding me into his arms. He carried me into my house and sat me down on the couch. Zeke and Ivan held the dogs back, letting them go one at a time. Each dog took a turn sniffing me, before nuzzling into my good leg. I took a moment to pet each of them. They circled the living room, finding places to lay down, their eyes watched me, looking sad.

"Since Sebastian and Alex are planning to be here, I don't figure we'll need more help. Do you want anything to eat?" Anthony looked at me.

"Yes." I looked at them. "Zeke insisted on stocking my kitchen with food, and if someone unloads the car we'll have cookware and towels."

"You? Have food?" Anthony smiled.
"There's a first time for everything."

"What do you want to eat?" Zeke headed for my kitchen.

"Almost-burnt bacon and hash browns." I told him.

I heard pans rattle. Anthony took a seat in one of my living room chairs. "How long are you supposed to go easy on your leg?"

"I don't know, I wasn't listening to the doctor, but I have instructions somewhere," I began going through my pockets; there was a tube of strawberry Chapstick, a serious amount of dog biscuit crumbles, pocket lint, an earring that I'd been missing for a couple of weeks, a sticker with a dragon on it whose origins were a complete mystery to me, a ball of unreadable paper mush that had been washed and dried at least once, a breath mint still in the wrapper, and a candy bar wrapper, but no instructions from the hospital. I checked the other pocket and there was nothing in it. "My guess is until I can do it without wanting to scream. I figure it's kind of like every other injury I've ever received. You take the first twenty-four hours and go easy on it, then start to use it a little more every day until its back to normal." Zeke handed me the piece of paper with the doctor's instructions. I folded them up and put them in my pocket.

"Nadine, I couldn't help but notice the big round scar on your leg when you were dressing.

What's that from?" Zeke asked as he walked back to the kitchen to check on the bacon sizzling on the stove. He turned to look at me through the bar.

"Tiger attack," I sighed, it would have to be explained. Anthony gave a snort, he already knew the story.

"Uh, do I want to hear this?" Zeke asked.

"Probably not. You can't seem to mix gross stories and food." I responded.

"Good thing I'm not eating then."

"Fine," I sighed, feeling tired and hungry. "I was working for an animal rescue center during the summer when I was in high school. My job was to make sure the habitats were free of trash and stuff. I had someone else with me and was cleaning out the tiger enclosure. The person with me was supposed to watch the tiger, let me know if he was getting too interested in us, so we could leave. I found a dead bird, flipped it over to pick it up and found maggots on it. I kind of freaked out, forgot where I was and took off running. I ran right towards the tiger, which was on the other side of the habitat. My running got it very interested in me and my fear peaked it even further. The person with me was also slacking just a bit. Anyway, I got close and he pounced; latched on to my thigh with his jaws and yanked. Luckily for me, he just tore away the skin and some muscle instead of dragging me. It left a ragged circle where he liberated a hunk of my leg. What I remember most is that it hurt, what I remember the least is how I got out of the tiger cage."

"That would..." Zeke thought for a moment, I knew he was groping for the right word. Everyone groped for a word to describe it. "Huh, I don't know what to say to that." He gave a small laugh. "What happened to the tiger?"

"Nothing, they wanted to put him down, but I did everything in my power to keep that from happening. In the end, a sign was hung up and a new enclosure built to ensure that the tiger was cordoned off when people were in his pen. I felt bad for the tiger, it wasn't his fault."

I ate my food quietly. When I finished, Anthony carried me up the stairs. I tucked myself into bed and closed my eyes. My limbs were still sore, but I was too tired to notice.

Melina Visits

Raucous laughter emanated from the downstairs, wrenching me from the narcotic-induced dreams I was having. I wasn't sure being woken up was a bad thing. I was sure that the laughter was, it belonged to my mother.

Dragging myself from bed, I looked at my pajamas. They covered all the important bits. They'd do to go downstairs and kick my mother out of my house. Of course, I wouldn't actually kick her out, that was impossible, but I would fantasize about it. The fantasy was always better than the reality anyway.

I limp-skipped to the top of the stairs. Once there, I just stared. Normally, I'd sit on my butt and just scoot down the stairs. However, my arm was also injured, so that didn't seem like an option. That left two options; limp skipping down them or yelling for help. I really didn't want to yell for help, but I figured I'd be back in the hospital if I attempted the other.

"Uh, could someone come get me?" I yelled down the stairs. Zeke appeared at the bottom. "Someone with more muscle?" Zeke was thin and muscular. Anthony was wide and muscular. Considering the feat included stairs, I wanted wide and muscular.

"I can carry you down a flight of steps," Zeke frowned at me.

"I'm sure you can, but I'm already injured so why take chances?" I asked. Zeke shook his head and walked up the stairs. He grabbed me, sweeping me off my feet, pivoted like a dancer, and we headed down the stairs. I closed my eyes for the adventure, not wanting to see the hardwood floor rushing up at me when we fell. With one movement, my feet were on the floor.

"See?" Zeke put me down on the floor without injury.

"Well, I'm shocked," I admitted. My mother was cooking. This was a really bad sign. My mother only cooked when she was up to something.

"Nadine," she cooed at me. I felt like throwing up, and I didn't think it was the narcotics or the pain.

"Mom, what are you doing?"

"Cooking," she spread her arms wide. "Alex and Sebastian are on their way. You girls have really gotten yourselves into a mess this time." I looked at Anthony. Anthony would not meet my gaze.

"We usually eat junk food and pizza on football days," I told her.

"I'm making pizza," she answered. It didn't smell like pizza. "Oh my goodness!" She suddenly shouted.

"What?" We all three turned and started looking around for some type of danger.

"Nadine Duscha Daniels! How could you?" She scolded me while walking towards me.

"I didn't do anything!" I defended myself, not sure what I was being accused of.

"You introduced him as your roommate!" My mother looked like she was going to cry. I was still confused.

"He is my roommate!" I looked at Zeke for help. He suddenly paled.

"You and your roommate wear matching wedding rings?" She snapped, grabbing my hand. I had forgotten all about the wedding ring. I was in trouble, thankfully, I was bringing Zeke with me.

"I can explain," I started.

"I can't believe you eloped!" She did start crying now. "Your grandfather will be so disappointed. And what about the rest of us? We didn't get to see you walk down the aisle or anything. Does Alex know about this? She does, doesn't she? She probably got to attend." My grandfather was a priest in the Russian Orthodox Church. He'd become a priest after leaving Russia. My grandmother had already died and he said he would never find another woman to love like her, so he took orders instead. My family might have a few crazy genes.

"Mom, I'm not married, this was just put on so that Zeke could sleep in my hospital room." I pulled at the ring, but it wouldn't come off.

"Are you ashamed because you eloped?" She narrowed her eyes at me. "We can make this right. I'll call your grandfather, and we'll make all the arrangements for a ceremony. No one has to know that you eloped."

"I'm not ashamed of eloping," I tried not to shout at her and took a deep breath to continue. In my family, eloping was probably the way to go.

"Is it because he's black?" My mother attempted to whisper this, but the cosmonauts on Sputnik could have heard her.

"What?" I stared at her. I didn't know how to answer that. She was Russian, there weren't a lot of black men in Russia. There also wasn't many that were Tahitian American, but she had lived in the US for the last forty years. We hadn't been raised in a house that acknowledged race, so I wasn't sure why she thought this was the problem.

"Love is love," she started.

"No, mom, it's not because he's black!" I did shout this. "It's because we did not get married. He really is my roommate."

"Oh no," she frowned at me, "you're the reason he got divorced, aren't you? You were the other woman. It started out as innocent flirting at work, then it became more serious and you started having an affair, didn't you? Are you pregnant? Is that why he left his wife?"

"What?" My mouth fell open, unable to imagine how she had made this leap of logic. Anthony was on his phone. I had a feeling he was texting someone. I wanted to plead for help, but I knew that would get me nowhere.

"Nadine," my mother took my hand. "You don't look pregnant, but we'll have to rush the wedding to make sure you're not showing when we do the ceremony."

"I'm not pregnant!" I shouted at her.

"He just left his wife for you?" She asked, her face an unreadable mask all of a sudden.

"No, mom, he didn't leave his wife for me."

"Technically, my wife kicked me out because she was having an affair," Zeke said. "I don't blame her, I was rarely home, we grew apart, and she fell in love with someone else."

"That's so sad," my mother's face turned sad again. "Then you found my Nadine." Zeke didn't say a word.

"Melina, listen to me very closely," I said. She was still holding my hand and the smile was back. "I am not pregnant. Zeke and I did not elope. We are not married. He is renting a room from me."

"How dare you call me Melina; I am your mother young lady."

"That's what you took from that statement?" I jerked my hand away and limped over to the wall. Leaning up against it, I texted Ivan. Ivan sent me a crying, laughing face emoticon back while my mother went on and on about arranging the ceremony.

"So you finally told your mother!" Alex shouted as she walked into the house. I wanted to kill her. She wandered into the room, Sebastian behind her, both were smiling.

"Tell her I didn't elope," I told Alex.

"Your mess." Alex's eyes were wet looking. She had recently laughed until she cried. I knew exactly who Anthony had been texting. I was going to kill them all. I turned to Zeke for help. Zeke's composure had returned. He relaxed against the back of the couch, and I was pretty sure he was also trying not to laugh. Everyone had gone insane.

The smoke alarm went off. The dogs began jumping and barking at the oven. Thick plumes of black smoke billowed from my stove. I wondered why I hadn't bought a replacement at the store the day before. I knew the answer; I hadn't intended to ever use the stove, so it should have been safe.

"Oh, the pizza!" My mother shouted and ran to the stove. She pulled it out. If it had been a pizza, it certainly wasn't now. Of course, I wasn't willing to bet it had been a pizza when she put it in the oven. She looked in the oven and pulled out a charred book, then a second book, then what might have been a magazine, finally she pulled out a bag that spilled extremely dry dog food on the floor as it crumbled to ash. "Nadine!" My mother used that tone.

"I don't use the oven," I shrugged at her. "I forgot about the books and magazine. There's probably a bag in there that used to contain them. I store the dog food in there because it's special dog food, and the dogs can't find it in there. I don't know why you didn't check the oven before you started using it."

"So it's my fault that the oven contained stuff that wasn't supposed to be cooked?" She put her hand on her hips.

"No, it's your fault for assuming I would use my oven as an oven and not as a special storage place for dog food." I thought about the books. "The books were in a plastic bag. Thanks, mom, you probably ruined my oven."

"Don't you dare make this my fault," that tone was back. "Why did you put a plastic bag in the oven?"

"I came in with the books and dog food and just shoved them all in the oven before the dogs swarmed me, then I forgot about them." I looked at the dog food. Pieces had blackened. "That's a sixty dollar bag of dog food. It's specially formulated for dogs with joint problems, but it seems to taste better than the normal dog food, because the Danes will eat the entire bag as soon as I bring it home. I have to mix it with their regular food. Now, I need a new bag," I sighed. I spent a ton of money on dog food. I never looked at the receipt because it would probably make me cry. Dogs should be tax write-offs.

"Good grief," my mother shook her head. The others were busy opening doors and windows despite it being February. I had to admit, it didn't smell good.

"I'll get delivery," Anthony said.

The Marriage Theory

"Why didn't you help me?" I asked Zeke after everyone left.

"Because I realized that nothing I could say or do was going to help. Face it, we're getting married, unless you can convince your mother otherwise." Zeke was munching on a leftover breadstick.

"You sound incredibly calm for a man condemned to marriage, especially to me."

"Well, I could panic, but it wouldn't do us any good. Besides, being married to you isn't the worst thing that could happen. You're smart, attractive, fun to be around, have your own money, can hold your own in a fight, and I already live here."

"So, you're just going to let my mother railroad us into getting married?"

"If we tell her we got divorced, it will make it worse for both of us. She'll hound us until we decide to kill people, possibly her." Zeke thought for a moment. "However, killing her won't do us any good, because we'll have my mother to deal with as well."

"You're mother? She lives in Tahiti."

"Do you know what I realized while you were arguing with your mother today?"

"No."

"She's a French-Tahitian carbon-copy of your mother. I imagine that the mothers will either love each other or hate each other. It doesn't really matter. As I watched you argue with your mother, it was like watching me argue with mine. Now, my mother hated my ex-wife. She made sure to let us both know about it too. She called her the Demon Wife. It's a big part of the reason I'm now divorced. However, I believe she'll like you."

"So, you're going to go through with the marriage to make your mother happy?"

"No, I'm going to go through with the marriage because I don't believe you can talk your way out of it. Besides, I liked being married. I came home and had someone to talk to. I had someone who appreciated my cooking. The biggest difference is that when I don't come home because I'm working, you'll know I'm really working and won't think I'm stepping out on you. There's something to be said for that too."

"What if I don't appreciate your cooking?"

"You'll learn," Zeke looked thoughtful for another moment. "And you like football, which is a huge bonus. My ex-wife didn't like any sports."

"Essentially, we're getting married because you won't help me set my mother straight."

"Exactly. Did you forget I said I had a mother just like her? I'm not crossing that woman. If she wants us to get married, I'll stand with you at the altar."

"You're a wuss."

"I am when it comes to women like our mothers." Zeke chewed for a second. "Maybe it's fate, we have mothers made from the same mold, enjoy similar things, live together, it might be the best marriage ever."

"You're still a wuss," I took a breadstick and sat down next to him. My phone rang. Alex's number showed up. I sent it to voicemail. Needless to say, I was still irritated with her. It rang again. Again, Alex's number flashed on the caller ID. Again, I sent it to voicemail.

"That could be important," Zeke said.

"Or she could be calling to laugh at me."

"She's laughing with you."

"I'm not laughing."

"Maybe not today, but in a few years, you'll wonder why you didn't marry me sooner."

"You think you're that good of a catch?" I raised an eyebrow as I sent my phone to voicemail yet again.

"No, Nadine, I don't. I just think that we have enough in common and enough differences that we won't drive each other crazy. Were your parents happily married?"

"Um, no," I said.

"Mine either. I kept waiting for my mom to kill my father."

"Me too."

"We're already a step ahead of their marriages." Zeke took my phone as it started to ring again. "She's pissed at you for not helping with her mother today. She's also pissed at me, but at least she understands my reasoning." He didn't offer a hello or anything else.

He listened for a few minutes. Nodding at the phone and making noises when appropriate. After another minute, he handed me the phone.

I stared at it in his hand, refusing to take it. He sighed and grabbed my hand, shoving the phone in it.

"What?" I snipped.

"Okay, it was funny at first, but now it's serious," Alex said. "Your mother is telling everyone. She even conned Lucy into giving her Zeke's mother's name and number. She called to tell her. I tried to tell her, and she told me to stop trying to ruin your happiness."

I put my head on the table. It was cool and hard to the touch. As Alex talked, I began hitting my head on the table. Not hard enough to draw blood, but I was sort of hoping it would cause sudden death. Zeke put his hand down and my forehead hit it. He also took the phone.

"Thanks, Alex. I guess I have to call my mother." He hung up. My front door banged open and then closed. Zeke went to draw his gun, removing his hand from the table. I began hitting it again.

"Holy crap, mom just told me she called Telisa and Telisa is pissed about the eloping thing. Granddad called me to figure out if I thought Zeke could be baptized in the Russian Orthodox

Church," Ivan paused. "Are you hitting your head on the table?"

Zeke shoved his hand back down. My forehead landed on it with a duller sounding thud. I didn't lift it.

"Yeah, Alex called. I think your sister is having a meltdown."

"Our mother is why Amy and I got married," Ivan sat down next to me. He pushed a bottle of whiskey my way. "Amy and I were dating, we'd been together six months. Our mother decided it was time to get married and next thing Amy and I knew, we were picking out place settings and arranging for caterers. We didn't even pick out the rings, Melina did. Melina managed to plan the wedding in less than a month. She even got Amy's parents involved. We didn't have a prayer."

I opened the whiskey and drank straight from the bottle. After the second swig, Ivan took the bottle from me. He took a slug and passed it to Zeke. Zeke shut off his phone and took a drink. Then he shut off my phone and handed me the bottle.

"So, how do we get out of this?" Zeke asked.

"Move, that's what Nadine's other boyfriends had to do," Ivan answered.

"Drink ourselves to death," I suggested, not passing the bottle to Ivan.

"Well, the good news is, our mother's arranged marriages seem to work. She's steam rolled three cousins and myself. We're all happy." Ivan yanked the bottle from my hands. "We have a brother that's the exception." "Lately she's been rethinking you and Amy," I told Ivan.

"I know, she told me about it." Ivan answered. "However, I'm not going to divorce her just because Melina says she is giving her creepy vibes."

"Oh man," Zeke took the bottle and drank half of it. "My mother has feelings about people too."

"What are you going to do?" Ivan asked. I looked at him.

"We're going to get married," Zeke told him. "I'm not moving, I like it here and I have a good job. I could do worse than Nadine for a wife. My mother isn't religious, so I've never been baptized, I might as well be Russian Orthodox. If your mother has told my mother," Zeke shrugged.

"Wuss," I muttered, feeling the effects of the whiskey and Vicodin.

"That would be correct," Zeke answered.

"Are you drunk?"

"Yes." I took the bottle and finished it off. Ivan produced another from an unknown location near his leg.

"I thought we might need several while we brainstormed ways to get you out of getting married." Ivan offered.

"I could get killed instead of kidnapped," I offered with a hiccup.

"This has just been boiled down to the base: death or marriage." Ivan brought out another bottle, setting it next to the other unopened one on the table. "I might need to go back to the liquor store."

Hangovers

In the morning, I felt like crap. I had passed out at my dining room table. Ivan and Zeke were still passed out. I thought about pointing out they were crappy body guards, but the truth was, I didn't care. They deserved to be passed out. I didn't remember most of the night. There were over a dozen whiskey bottles scattered around the room.

Even more surprising, Alex and Sebastian were both passed out in my living room. At some point, we had called in reinforcements, probably for the booze and not our protection. Anubis, my largest Great Dane, let out a small yowl. There was an empty bottle of whiskey next to him. He stood up, took two steps, and face planted. My dog was drunk. He flopped onto his side and let out the yowl again. It was a sound I had never heard from him.

Marduk, his brother, answered the yowl with a similar noise. Baldur got to his feet and staggered to the water bowl. He lapped at the water, one foot off the ground, his butt slightly lower than the rest of his body.

"The Great Danes are drunk!" I shouted.

"Jeez, Nadine," Ivan groaned.

"My dogs are drunk. How did my dogs get drunk?" I asked.

"I don't remember," Ivan answered. "I don't remember much after Alex called me. Did they ever come over?"

"Yes," I kicked Alex's leg. She groaned. "My dogs are drunk."

"It was your idea," she rolled over. "You're the one that gave Anubis an open bottle to commiserate with us about your upcoming nuptials."

"Wow!" Anthony walked into the room. I hadn't heard him enter. My dogs all yowled again. "Are they drunk?"

"Yes," I snapped at him. "In theory, it was my idea. I feel bad for them."

"You should feel bad for yourself. Your mother is going to pick out invitations this afternoon. You're getting married on Valentine's Day." Anthony told us.

"That's impossible. It's January. These things take time." I told him.

"Not with your mother." Anthony looked around. "Oh, I'm guessing that's what the whiskey was about."

"Yes," Zeke stood up. "We realized we couldn't talk her out of it, so Ivan came over with whiskey. She's done this before."

"I know," Anthony answered. "Hangover breakfasts?"

"If I eat, I'll die," Ivan told him. "I need to call work and Amy."

"That's why I'm here," Anthony said. "Amy called and asked me to check on you. She's the one that told me about Melina picking out invitations today. Amy called work for you and said there was a family emergency. Zeke, you good?"

"I'm great," he started singing *I'm Getting Married in the Morning.*

"Stop or I'll shoot you," I told him. "If you keep shouting, I'm going to shoot you too. And we are not having breakfast, my head cannot stand the idea of pots and pans banging around. I don't think the reality will be any easier on me." I glared at Anthony. He smiled back.

"Hey, if she shoots you, you might be able to get out of the wedding," Ivan offered.

"Is there any more whiskey?" I asked.

"No, the dogs finished off all the bottles," Sebastian sat up on my living room floor. "After everyone passed out, there were a couple of bottles left. Anubis, having had a taste, decided he wanted more. They managed to figure out how to open the bottles."

"How do you know that?" I asked Sebastian.

"Because I didn't drink like you guys," Sebastian looked at me. "I had three shots, and I can handle that. I did attempt to take the bottles away from the dogs, but Baldur snapped at me."

"That explains why they are all drunk," Zeke shrugged. He turned his phone on. After about thirty seconds, it began sending alerts faster than my head could handle. He paled again.

"Zeke? What's wrong?" Alex asked.

"My mother is on a plane, headed here," Zeke turned his phone towards me. I read the text message and hung my head. I was fairly certain this day could not get any worse.

"Okay, ignoring Zeke and I's wedding for a moment, have we made any progress with Amanda Reed?" I asked.

"Kenzie has tracked her to somewhere in Spain," Anthony said. "She hopped on a plane before the whole incident with your mother happened."

"We've got the husband in protective custody. He's willing to turn on the mob to save his skin. The US Marshals pick him up today." Ivan told me. "However, until you find the mob's money or Amanda Reed, they are going to keep coming after you."

"Well, they can deal with my mother," I snapped at him. It actually wasn't a bad idea. She'd made stronger men cry. I was getting married because of her. She really was a force of nature. I'd give them to her and they might decide the money wasn't worth it.

"We could start a war," Anthony offered. "It would buy us some time. If the Russians find out that the Italians are trying to kill you, it might piss off the Russians enough to cause some friction."

"I think we'll use that as a last resort." My family had been in all sorts of things; they were members of the KGB, Spetznaz, and now the new Russian police. The Russian Mob didn't like us very much. To make it worse, my mother had once brokered a deal between the Russian Mob and the

CIA in a sting operation. It was why the Russians had tried to kill me, on more than one occasion. However, in recent years they had backed off because my family in Russia was just as determined as my family in the US. My mother's brother had moved to the top of the ranks and loved busting down the doors of mobsters. His son did it too, but wasn't a cop. He was more like Anthony. It never ended well for the mob when my cousin, Vasili, came into their houses. "See if Vasili can meet with Kenzie in Spain."

"Kenzie and Vasili?" Alex looked at me. Alex was my first cousin on my mother's side. Kenzie was my first cousin on my father's side. However, they were friends with each other and knew each other well. Kenzie would have made an excellent Russian woman.

"We need resources, Vasili is a resource," I looked at Alex. "The worst that can happen is Vasili gets tasered or hit with a hammer. He'll complain about it, but I'll just give him more money and the problem will be solved."

"Or Kenzie marries him and he becomes ex number six," Alex said. Kenzie had been married and divorced five times, despite being only a year older than me. She had no children and despite owning a thriving business, she was always broke because of alimony.

"She's never been attracted to Russian men and Vasili is definitely Russian," I shrugged. "I don't have any other ideas. If you do, I'm all ears." Alex was quiet.

"Then I think I should go too," Anthony said. He frowned. "If the lot of you think you can keep from having a repeat drunk fest, that is."

"No promises," I told him. "Just wait, one day, my mother will sink her claws into you, and you'll be the one getting married."

"I am aware of that possibility," Anthony grabbed his phone and called Lucy. Lucy called back after a few moments to give him the itinerary. "So, breakfast?"

"Good lord," I groaned. Baldur was passed out on the stairs. Loki was passed out a few steps further up. There was no way I was getting up them. "I can't get upstairs to change."

"Yes, but now you have pans, so we can cook," Anthony told me.

"You guys cook," I looked at the clock. "I'm going to go make calls."

"Who are you calling?"

"Devlin, Vladik, and Liam," I answered.

"They already know."

"I expect them to know; I'm hoping they have a way out of this mess." I told him.

"Which mess?" Ivan asked.

"Well, they all work for agencies with initials, not names. Maybe they can give me something on Amanda Reed," I started dialing Liam. "If not, maybe they can help me and Zeke disappear before our mothers meet."

The three brothers smart enough to move away were no help. They wouldn't abuse their positions to find out information about Amanda, although Liam was interested in the mob angle, since he worked for the FBI. Not one of them had a single clue what to do about my getting married. They all wished me luck and said they were requesting time off to attend.

My phone rang. The number that came up made my stomach churn. It was my cousin, Katya. Katya's parents owned a furniture store. I was sure she was calling to congratulate me on the wedding.

"Hello, Katya," I answered.

"Nadine, I'm so happy for you," she said with a slight accent. Most of my cousins were first generation Americans. That meant most of them still had Russian accents and spoke in Russian when it suited them.

"Thanks, Katya," I leaned my head against the wall.

"Your mother called and said there was an incident with the stove," Katya continued. "So, we send you new stove! Our men will be delivering it today." Katya's voice was lyrical and excited. I wanted to cry. I settled for beating my head against the wall. My forehead was going to become bruised at this rate.

"Thank you, Katya," I banged my head against the wall in time with the syllables of the words coming from my mouth. "The stove will be a great gift. Thank Natasha and Mikhail for me."

"I will!" Katya paused for a moment, "we send black one, is that okay?"

"Black is fine," I answered.

"I hear your fiancé has very blue eyes, very pretty to look at."

"Yes, Katya, he does have very blue eyes and they are very pretty to look at. They are an ice blue most of the time," I hung up. Ivan stopped me banging my head, which I had forgot I was doing.

"The first wedding gift?" Ivan asked.

"A new stove," I answered. "For some reason, I don't care much about being stabbed. I wish he had done a better job."

"That's how I felt too. It gets better. Zeke's a good guy. He'll make you happy. Unless you aren't sexually attracted to him, then you guys are going to have to make some sort of arrangements." Ivan frowned.

"I'm still trying to figure out how to walk down the aisle. Can we not talk about sex? Why did she pick Valentine's Day? Isn't that tacky?"

"Yes, but she knew you would remember your anniversary if it was also a holiday and New Year's has passed."

I frowned. Ivan was right. I would remember it.

The Arrival

If there was any justice in the world, the mob would attack my house within the hour. Unfortunately, I had never had that kind of luck. They only attacked when I didn't want them to, never when it would have been helpful.

My mother was in her Sunday finest, despite it being Friday evening. This meant a skirt suit worth more than my couch and hooker shoes. I had no idea why she was obsessed with stiletto heels, considering she was in her sixties, but she never seemed to be without a pair. The only purpose I could find for them was stabbing people if I needed a make-shift weapon.

Her long nails were painted a bright purple with wavy lines in a lighter purple. I didn't have a name for either shade of purple. Nor did I understand how the wavy lines got put on. Once, when I had been ten, my mother had taken me to get a manicure. She'd picked yellow for the color, and it had lasted until we got home. As soon as I got in the door, I had found the finger nail polish remover and scrubbed it off. It had already started chipping anyway. She had given up on making me a girly girl after that. She didn't seem to understand that with four brothers, two older and two younger, it was hard to be a girly girl and not get picked on.

Zeke was on his way to get his mother from the airport. Alex and Sebastian were forced to join us for this first meet and greet, since I needed body guards and Daniels' Security Agency was running low. I couldn't keep up with business even when I wasn't in need of a personal guard. I made a mental note to hire more staff. There was no doubt that I would forget it within the hour.

"So, what do you know about Telisa?" Melina asked me.

"Not a thing. Until yesterday, I wouldn't have even been able to tell you if he had a mother," I hiccupped. I was still a little hungover. My dogs were sleeping it off. I envied them.

"Nadine," my mother used that tone when saying my name. "Don't be ridiculous. Everyone has a mother."

"Alex doesn't," I pointed out.

"Yes she does," my mother gave me a look that would have stopped me dead if a mother's stares worked that way. While Alex did technically have a mother, she had never met her. Her mother had run-off after giving birth. Her father had gone back to Russia. My parents had raised her after that. All Alex and I knew about her mother was that she had been Russian born and married to my mother's brother, Boris. "That was very insensitive of you," my mother leaned in to whisper, but as usual, my mother's whispers could be heard in outer space. If NASA had really wanted to find life on other planets, they could just give my mother a megaphone and tell her to shout at the stars. Of course, this would probably lead to an invasion, because my mother had a habit of being offensive without meaning to be.

"Are you going deaf?" I asked her. "When you whisper, people in the next house over can hear you."

"I absolutely am not losing my hearing, Nadine Daniels." My mother huffed at me. "And I will thank you to keep your offensive remarks to yourself. Never would I have talked to my mother in such a way." This was probably true. My family was like most Russian families, the women were in charge. While society as a whole was patriarchal, there was this mythology built around females that kept them from being second class citizens. In some ways, they had far more power, skills and good old fashioned determination, than any Russian male could ever hope to achieve. The difference between my family and other Russian families was that my family seemed to have a double-dose of female willpower. If one wanted proof, they need look no further than my great-aunt Olga.

"So, what are the bridesmaids wearing?" Alex asked. I gave her my own version of my mother's deadly glare. My mother instantly became personable again. It was hard to trust someone who had mood swings and wore hooker heels. In the years since my father's death, my mother had changed, a lot. During my youth, I would never have seen her in such high heels, she wore more sensible shoes. She dressed nicely, but conservatively. Sometimes I wondered if she was advertising the fact that she was single, or if this was the real her and she had just stifled it while married.

"With Kenzie being in the wedding, we will need something soft," my mother started talking.

"Who said Kenzie's in the wedding?" I asked. She would be, if I got married, but that was for me to decide, not my mother.

"Don't be ridiculous," my mother scoffed at me. Obviously, I was wrong and had no say in the matter. "As I was saying, with Kenzie we will need soft colors, her fair skin will look terrible in yellow or a dark green. I am considering a light blue, to match Zeke's eyes, accented with an even lighter pink." I suddenly realized how Katya knew Zeke had blue eyes. Maybe Zeke was my mom's idea of good looking and marrying me off to him removed the temptation that she was feeling. It sounded twisted, but twisted summed up my family.

Despite the fact that they were planning my wedding, I felt like I was twelve. I was totally unnecessary even though the arrangements being made impacted my life the most. My forehead hurt from hitting the wall earlier, or I would have banged it a few more times.

"Nadine, why didn't you shower this morning? You have dirty spots on your forehead," my mother stood up, rushed to the kitchen and grabbed a paper towel. Before I could stop her, she was scrubbing my forehead. I was sure this was just making the bruise worse.

The sound of a car stopped the forehead scrubbing. I checked the clock. Zeke had been gone two hours. That was plenty of time to pick up his mother and get back here. Nervousness set in. I struggled to hold down my lunch and gave the room one last look for any small drop of whiskey that might have been left. At this point, it could have been one of the dogs' bottles, and I wouldn't have cared.

It suddenly sounded as if someone started throwing giant firecrackers at my house. Despite the bum leg, I dove at my mother, taking her to the ground. Something hard pressed into my chest. Sebastian and Alex were crawling towards the front hall.

My mother squirmed out from under me and also began a belly crawl towards the front of my house. She had a huge handgun that I was sure wasn't legal in her hands. My gun was upstairs. My dogs, disturbed by the noise, woke up.

Baldur growled. He found his footing and moved towards the utility room. Anubis followed, a little less enthusiastically. They could get out that door. All my dogs were trained, despite not acting like it. They took commands in German and they could get mean. Anubis was the largest, standing forty-two inches tall and weighing nearly two hundred pounds. However, none of them were registered as they were all too tall at the withers to be AKC registrable. Loki got to his feet, a little less steadily than the others. His eyes were redder than normal. Drool hung from his bottom lip. He went into the utility room. Enki, the smallest of the six, by four inches and thirty pounds, huffed out his jowls before joining his brothers. Marduk was the only one that stayed.

Suddenly, I wasn't sure if the shooter should be more afraid of my mother or my dogs. My house was set up a little strange, the entrance way was actually a room that might once have been a parlor or something. My mother had made her way into this room and was taking up a position near a window. Glass tinkled as one of the windows broke, sending glass skittering across the hardwood floors.

Sebastian was making hand gestures to my mother and Alex. Both seemed to be ignoring him. My mother fired back, taking a two handed grip on her gun, it still jerked her wrists with the recoil. Someone outside shouted.

I considered my options. I could stay on the floor of the living room and watch my friends and my mother fight the bad guys, or I could try to help. I looked at Marduk. The Dane seemed to sigh at me as he padded by on his large paws.

Suddenly, all hell broke loose. The gunshots stopped, but they were replaced by screaming. Some of the screams were very high pitched. Sebastian threw open the front door and was gone. I dialed 911.

"911, do you need fire, police, or rescue?" A woman's voice came on the line. It was very pleasant, as Alex would say, she gave good phone.

"All three, this is Nadine Daniels and there is at least one person, possibly more, shooting at my house," I answered.

"Miss Daniels, I am dispatching officers and EMS now," the operator told me.

"Great, how long?"

"A few minutes, it appears there is a detective responding as well." The operator sounded a little confused.

"That would be my brother." The day was not getting any better. "You might warn officers that there are six large Great Danes on the property; they are trained, and currently they are outside." I thought about Zeke, someone should really call him. "Mom, stop shooting at people and call Zeke."

"You call Zeke," my mother replied, firing again with the giant handgun. I sighed.

"Are you returning fire?" The operator asked.

"I'm not, no, but my mother, a private detective and security agent is. I was kidnapped and stabbed two days ago." There was a clicking noise.

"Miss Daniels, this is Officer Diego Vasquez. Did you say your mother was returning fire?" There was a hint of laughter in his voice. Diego Vasquez was about my age, he and my younger brother were very good friends in school. They still kept in touch. He knew my mother.

"Yes. Are you a responding officer?" I asked.

"Yes," he answered.

"Good," I hung up with 911 and called him directly on his cell phone. He answered on the first ring. "The guys outside might be mob related."

"Italian Mob or Russian Mob?" Diego asked.

"Italian," I answered. "They've stopped shooting, but I can still hear shouting, so I imagine they are outnumbered by the Danes. Please don't shoot my dogs."

"Your mother is firing at them even though they aren't shooting?"

"Yes and Sebastian ran out the door about a minute ago, so I don't know what he's doing either. I'm kind of hoping he isn't dead."

"Good grief," Diego let out a long sigh. I understood. "Tell your mother to hide the gun, I know she doesn't have a permit."

"Isn't that illegal?"

"Just do it, I'm almost there," Diego hung up.

"Mom, Diego Vasquez is one of the responding officers. He said to stop shooting at them, since you don't have a permit for your gun."

"Well, you just wait until I see him," she put away her gun. "They attacked us; we have a right to defend ourselves. I've read the constitution."

"Yes, mom," I let out my own long sigh as sirens approached. I was tempted to start banging my head against the wall again, bruised or not.

The Other Arrival

Officer Diego Vasquez was a just under six feet tall. He had brown hair, blue eyes, and fair skin. He was standing next to me. The detective turned out not to be Ivan. Ivan had called though, which was when I remembered his wife had called in sick for him.

We had a detective named Jim Jones, which kind of made me feel sorry for him. Even if I had thought of a Kool-Aid joke, I was sure he got them more often than he wanted. If that hadn't done it, it would be his current predicament, in theory, he was supposed to be questioning my mother. In reality, my mother was lecturing him about how to groom his facial hair, which she found untidy and was therefore the sole reason Detective James Jones did not have a wedding ring on his finger.

Sebastian was talking to another officer, giving his statement. Luckily for his officer, Sebastian didn't care about marriage or grooming habits. He had seen two shooters. Both had taken off when they had been charged by six Great Danes. For some reason, big dogs just terrified some people. The shooters had abandoned their car and one of their guns, so I was guessing they were among those people terrified of big dogs. Baldur did have a piece of clothing in his mouth. He had given it to Diego Vasquez only after I had issued him some commands.

However, I was guessing the dogs were still hungover since they hadn't given chase. They usually loved to run, and chasing bad guys was just as fun as chasing anything else to them. I was just glad they were scary looking enough to send bad guys running away.

"When he comes and talks to you, you're going to play stupid, aren't you?" Diego Vasquez asked.

"Yep," I answered, watching Jones. "Although, by the time my mother gets done with him, he might have a nervous breakdown."

"I'm pretty sure she just used the word manscaping," Diego looked at me.

"I'm trying not to listen." I shrugged.

"Congrats on getting married by the way," Diego offered.

"Thanks, it's her fault. Zeke is picking…" I remembered I hadn't called Zeke. "Dang, I forgot to let Zeke know about all this. He's picking up his mother from the airport."

"Wow, your mother and your mother-in-law," Diego gave a small whistle.

"Yep, I'd rather deal with mobsters."

"We have a K-9 unit on the way."

"Great, my dogs seem too hungover to care a whole lot about tracking down bad guys."

"Your dogs were drunk?"

"My dogs might still be drunk, I'm not really sure. They finished a couple of bottles of whiskey last night. Everyone was too drunk to put them out of their reach." I sighed. "We were having a pity party because Zeke and I are getting married."

"I didn't know the two of you were dating."

"We aren't," I answered. "He needed a place to stay, I rented him a room, then I was kidnapped, and now my mother is convinced we eloped. So, she is planning a ceremony at my grandfather's church and keeping the elopement secret."

"What is she going to do when she finds out there isn't a marriage certificate on file for you?"

"Probably file one." I hadn't thought of that. "You know how she gets."

"Yeah, she's a riot," Diego smiled. I wondered if he'd lost his mind. "I hope you intend to send me an invitation."

"Sure," I answered. Detective Jones was now rubbing his eye. Either he had an eye twitch or was getting a headache, from this distance, I couldn't tell.

"Sergeant?" Another officer came running down my driveway. The sergeant in charge was Mike Williams. I'd meet him a few times before, sometimes because of my brother, sometimes because of situations like this. "Sergeant?" The officer shouted again.

"What?" Williams asked.

"I got a host of people at the end of the driveway and they aren't happy and they aren't speaking English. I don't know what it is. One of them is a box van with two big guys and a young woman, one is an SUV with a very vocal woman who might have sworn at me in French with a man who claims he lives here, and another car with a guy who says he's Secret Service, but is talking in a foreign language to the box van occupants. What should I do?" The officer asked.

"Those are for me," I held up my hand. I wasn't sure about the box van, but if they were talking to someone in a foreign language that had a Secret Service badge, they had to be family. "Secret Service guy is Liam Daniels, my older brother. Guy in SUV with a woman who is swearing is my fiancé, Ezekiel Laroche, the woman is his mother, so it's probably French. Box van is possibly family."

"It says Kazakhov Appliances and Furniture," the officer said.

"That would be my new stove," I thought for a moment. "Since my kitchen wasn't damaged, I see no reason not to have it delivered. I just hadn't expected it today." Katya had called me just this morning, they must have had one in stock. After these words left my mouth, I shut it and stood there, stunned. My house had bullet holes in it. There was an abandoned car in my driveway. My dogs were hungover. I was getting married. People wanted me dead. My mother had been shooting at people with an extremely large handgun that was probably of Russian origin and illegal. My Irish cousin was in Spain with my German assassin turned good guy and my Russian cousin who also happened to be a mercenary. Yet, I was taking delivery of a new stove with the police still in my drive way. At some point, my life had gone off the rails and the weird stuff no longer bothered me. That in itself should have bothered me.

"Nadine!" My brother was shouting my name as he came down the drive. Considering he had been working in Washington DC the day before, I was guessing my call had bothered him. Or maybe it was our mother's call that bothered him.

"Liam," I smiled at him. "What are you doing here?"

"I have a lot of vacation time saved up, it sounded like you might need help."

"No, I think everything is under control," I told him.

"Really?" Liam frowned and looked around. "It looks under control." I didn't appreciate his sarcasm.

"Hey, Liam," Diego Vasquez shook hands with my older brother. "How's it going?"

"I'd be better if I knew what was going on with my little sister."

"The usual," Diego shrugged. "You know how she is sometimes."

"That's what worries me," Liam looked at me again. "Marriage?"

"Ok, are you more worried about the shooting or the wedding?" I asked.

"You own a security agency, I believe the shooting is covered. No one died." Liam sneakily gestured towards our mother.

"Well, if you can convince mom that Zeke and I didn't elope, that would be helpful," I told him.

"You'd be better off having Zeke move."

"You are the second person to say that." I looked at Liam. He wasn't here because I was getting married. That would be a source of entertainment for him, as long as the guy was worthy. He knew something and I was going to have to wait for the police to leave to figure out what that was.

"Miss Daniels?" Detective Jones walked over to me. "Have you given a statement?"

"I gave one to Officer Vasquez," I answered. My statement had been very short and had consisted mostly of talk about my wedding.

"Can you think of why someone would want to shoot at you?" Detective Jones looked tired. He had aged significantly while talking to my mother.

"I own the most successful private security firm in the US. If you'd like, I can have my secretary send you a list of people who would like to kill me. That's why I have six Great Danes. However, I was kidnapped the day before last by Fred Reed. His wife Amanda disappeared last year, for some reason, he thinks I'm involved."

"Are you?"

"Involved in the disappearance of Amanda Reed?" I looked at him for a second. I could lie and it would be somewhat believable. I could tell the truth and stir up a storm. "Yes." My brother shook his head.

"You were involved with the disappearance of Amanda Reed?" Detective Jones asked me again.

"Yes," I answered. "She hired my company for protective services. She said it was a stalker. It turned out to be her husband and the mob. We terminated our contract with her and she went missing the following day."

"I'm confused. You terminated your services, but made her disappear?" Detective Jones frowned.

"No, we terminated our contract with her, and she went missing after that. If we had not terminated our contract, she wouldn't have disappeared." I answered.

"Then the correct answer is no, you didn't make Amanda Reed disappear," Detective Jones looked a little more tired.

"I guess that depends on how you look at the situation," I answered. "Responsibility is responsibility. If I give my keys to a twelve year old and that kid hits someone and kills them, I am still responsible for that death."

"Maybe you should have a talk with your mother about the finer points of law. Feeling responsible doesn't make you guilty of committing a crime," Detective Jones finished talking and walked away.

"Wow," Vasquez said after a moment. "That was masterful."

"I told the truth," I countered.

"And yet, manipulated him into believing the lie without ever stating the lie," Vasquez commented. "I really am impressed." Vasquez knew that Alex and I ran a sort of escape system for people stuck in bad situations. We'd helped dozens of people escape abusive relationships, gangs and a host of situations that resulted in people being a victim of circumstance.

"Who's that with Zeke?" Liam asked.

"His mother," I took a deep breath. "This is probably not going to impress my future mother-in-law."

Tahiti Meets Russia

Most people meet their future mother-in-law at a dinner or luncheon. Not me, I was getting to meet mine with police in my driveway. There were also two burly Russian men arguing in Russian on my lawn about the best way to move a stove from the road, where it sat in a truck, to my kitchen. A pretty blonde Russian woman was playing mediator, however, I was fairly certain Katya was more interested in the tall man that was walking down my drive with his mother.

Zeke wasn't running, but his movements were awkward, giving the impression that he might have considered it. His mother was moving at a fast clip beside him. As they got closer, I found Zeke had inherited his ice blue eyes from his mother.

Telisa Laroche was a beautiful woman. She was tall with skin the color of coffee with just a hint of creamer. Her hair was pulled up in a large scrunchy or some sort of fancy hair piece that created a wild mass of spiral curls. There wasn't a hint of grey in it. Zeke kept his head shaved or stubbled, and I wondered if he had her curls as well. He was a little lighter skinned than her, but the resemblance was definitely there.

As my mother took a step closer to me, Liam took a step away. Sebastian and Alex were behind us. My stomach knotted again. I wasn't entirely sure why I wanted this woman to like me, but I did and I was positive I wasn't making a good first impression.

"Are you okay?" Zeke asked as he came up to me.

"Yeah, we're all fine. The dogs took care of them," I stammered in a barely audible hiss of a voice. I cleared my throat. "We're good." This time it was louder and sounded more assured.

"Nadine, this is my mother, Telisa." Zeke pointed to his mother. "Mom, this is Nadine."

"I have heard such good things about you," Telisa hugged me. Her voice carried a thick accent that made it sound lyrical. "Even when he was married to that other woman, my son spoke highly of you. Are you sure you're alright, dear?"

"Yes, we're fine," I repeated. "Let me introduce some of my family. I apologize for overwhelming you after stepping off a plane, but they were here for security purposes. This is my mother, Melina, my brother, Liam, my cousin, Alexandra, one of my employees, Sebastian, and I have another brother on the way, Ivan."

"Sebastian," Telisa walked over and hugged him. "We have met before." Telisa then walked over to Melina. The two women looked at each other for a moment, not saying a word. I was waiting for them to break out nunchakus and start brawling. Instead, they shook hands, clasping each other's hands in a warm gesture. It was strange to watch. My mother wasn't the friendliest person. Zeke looked a little confused and a little concerned as well.

"I think they are done with us, so we should go inside," I pointed to the door with bullet holes in it. "I'll call a handyman I know to come sort this all out." My security firm kept two handymen on staff for situations just like this.

"Nadine, where do we put this?" Katya pointed to her brothers, they were carrying my new stove.

"Oh, uh, follow me," I led Katya, Dmitri and Petyr into the house. Everyone else followed behind them. Dmitri and Petyr disconnected everything on the old stove and connected everything on the new stove while we stood awkwardly around and watched.

"I'm Katya," Katya introduced herself to Zeke and Telisa. "Nadine and Alex are our cousins." She pointed to her brothers as she said this last part. Zeke and Telisa both shook Katya's extended hand. "We have a big family. It is wonderful." I rolled my eyes at that statement. Wonderful was not an adjective I would have used to describe our family.

"Wedding gift installed!" Dmitri announced with a flourish of his arms and a raising of his voice. He came over and hugged me, pulling me off my feet. Then he walked over and hugged Zeke, doing the same thing. Petyr followed his brother's example, and I found myself once again being hugged. That was the third time today. I wondered if it was one of the signs of the apocalypse.

Dmitri, Petyr and Katya left, although Katya kept trying to find excuses to stay. I got the impression she was kind of enamored by my unlikely fiancé. After they left, the awkwardness drained a little and we all moved into the living room. Melina and Telisa arranged it so Zeke and I had to sit next to each other. Zeke was right, they were a lot alike.

"Now, tell me children, what have you gotten yourselves into?" Telisa asked.

"Um," I frowned, not sure if she meant the shooting or the wedding. I was finding those two things seemed to overlap each other.

"One of Nadine and Alex's special jobs," Zeke said. "It's coming back to haunt them. We have a few people looking for the person in question, but we haven't had much luck. We've tracked them to Spain, which is where Anthony is."

"Has everyone at the office but me met your mother?" I whispered.

"Yes," Telisa answered for Zeke. "But not for lack of trying. I have been trying to meet you for a while. First it was just because Zeke loved his job, but then I realized he was falling in love with you, because he talked about you all the time. Now, I'm glad you two are finally together and I get to meet you. I feel like I already know you!"

"Oh," I smiled at her, unsure what else to say. Could it be possible that Zeke had been in love with me? I'd have to ask.

"Now that I'm here, I'm going to stay until the wedding, I wanted to take a vacation from the island anyway," Telisa said.

"Where are you staying?" Melina asked.

"Zeke said I could stay here, but I know young couples, and I don't want to be in their way. I was looking at long stay hotels." Telisa answered.

"Don't be silly," my mother tutted her. I wondered if Telisa would kill her. She didn't. She didn't even seem to mind. "You will stay with me. We will have so much to do anyway and we need to get better acquainted. Although, after talking to you yesterday, I feel like I've known you all my life."

"Me too!" Telisa smiled wide, her eyes sparkled.

"How long did you two talk on the phone yesterday?" I asked.

"Four hours or so," Melina answered. I had nothing to say to that, at least, nothing that wouldn't get me in trouble, so I kept my mouth shut.

"I'm going to go check in with Anthony," Sebastian announced loudly.

"I'll go with you," Alex stood up and followed him upstairs.

Liam didn't move. He stared at our mother. He opened his mouth and I gently prodded him. Now was not the time. He glared at me.

"Mom, they didn't elope," Liam announced. "They aren't engaged. Nadine is just renting Zeke a room."

"What did you say about cantaloupe? It's winter, it's hard to get good cantaloupe this time of the year. They are always a little bitter." Melina didn't even look at Liam. She was busy talking to Telisa.

"No, mom, not married," Liam said.

"What?" My mother turned to look at him, fire sparked in her eyes. "What do you mean you aren't married? You were married when I talked to you yesterday. Did you leave her or did she leave you? What did she do? Where are the children?"

"Not me, them," Liam pointed at Zeke and I.

"Yes, Liam, that's why we're having a ceremony," my mother brushed him off at that comment, returning to her conversation with Telisa. It was currently centered on wedding cakes. Liam looked confused now. He hung his head and shook it.

"Yep, selectively deaf," I whispered to my brother.

"I tried. At least Zeke's a good guy, he was genuinely concerned about you when he showed up and found you'd been shot at." Liam gave me a sad, sympathetic look. Liam, like Ivan, had been railroaded by our mother into marriage. It had started as a social event and ended up being a secret setup. After six months, our mother was insisting they marry. Then we all woke up one morning with invitations to the wedding. Unlike Ivan, Liam was not happily married. His wife was a harpy. My mother hated the woman now.

Both women suddenly started talking in French. I didn't know my mother knew French. She pulled her gun out of her purse and showed it to Telisa. Telisa was appropriately impressed. Our mothers were bonding over forced weddings and handguns. Everything was just peachy.

Amanda Reed

The handyman showed up to temporarily fix the house. He'd come back during normal business hours and do a better job of it. Telisa and Melina were cooking in my kitchen, chatting like old friends. Liam motioned for us to move upstairs.

Sebastian and Alex were sitting on the floor in the spare room playing cards. They looked up at us with guilty looks when we walked in. Alex put her cards down.

"So?" She asked.

"Oh, it's just dandy, they love each other," I sighed and flopped onto the bed.

"I told you she was just like your mother, you didn't believe me, but she is," Zeke answered.

"Oh, yeah, I'm understanding it now." I snarked at him.

"Hey, I warned you, and I didn't invite her here, your mother did that."

"Ah, your first couple's fight, how cute," Sebastian cooed.

"I'll kill you," I told him.

"I believe that." Sebastian put his own cards down. "Anthony hasn't arrived in Spain yet."

"So, you've just been hiding up here, playing cards?" Zeke asked.

"Yes," Alex answered. "Telisa is like Melina. How many of your siblings are married?"

"All of them," Zeke answered. "And before you ask, my mom had a hand in all of them. She's part witch doctor, part crazy person, part mother."

"What are we going to do if they don't find Amanda Reed soon?" I decided I couldn't talk about our mothers any longer. It was creeping me out.

"You're going to owe one of your brothers, big time," Liam answered. "That's why I'm here. Devlin has a lead for them to follow. A woman named Lydia Barnes arrived in Spain about two months ago, but she didn't exist until her passport was checked in Spain. She matches the description of your girl, but there's a huge problem."

"Sounds about right," I commented.

"Devlin's agency is tracking her because they think she's involved in organized crime outside the country. They think she has been for a while, far longer than she's been missing. Amanda Reed has a college friend that got married and moved to Spain. They know the college friend's husband is involved in some shady stuff. The theory is that Amanda got involved and then Fred got involved." Liam told me.

"None of this showed up when we ran her," Alex said.

"It's all been confidential. Devlin says that his bosses are of the opinion that her criminal connections got her the new identity. If they find out otherwise, you two are going to be in a lot of trouble."

"Good grief," Alex sighed. "This is a disaster."

"There's a plan," Liam said. "Vladik, Anthony and Vasilii are working on it now. I'm here to make sure you stay alive until then."

"That can't be good," I looked at Liam. "If Vasilii is involved, someone's dying."

"That is not in the plan," Liam answered.

"Are you going to tell us the plan?" I asked.

"No," Liam answered. "Vlad is going to tell Zeke though."

"Why?" I asked.

"Because I'm secret service and, therefore, I can't know it. I can only know a small portion of it, the portion that isn't illegal. Which means I know that Vlad, Anthony, and Vasilii are meeting in Spain and then Vlad is coming here while Anthony and Vasilii go to Russia. Vlad came up with it. He has more wiggle room than the rest of us in the law and order department. He's going to fill in those that need to know. It's all about plausible deniability. If everything goes well, Amanda Reed comes back to the US to stand trial under RICO statutes, as does her college friend and Fred. The mob loses a connection in Spain."

"That's great, except I'm pretty sure that was the mob today," I pointed to the outside.

"I know," Liam pursed his lips.

"Well if we aren't blaming the Italian mob for Amanda Reed's disappearance," I stopped talking. Before I or my brothers were born, my mother was a double agent. She worked for the KGB and the CIA. It was how and why she had moved to the US and married our Irish father. Several members of our family moved to the US that way. Our Russian relatives were all involved in law enforcement agencies in Russia. This should have been a problem, but it wasn't, because of our maternal grandmother. She was a prominent, important

Russian who died in Russia after receiving just about every medal the USSR had to offer women.

In the 1980's, as the power of the Soviet Union declined, the KGB declined with it and some agents began working both sides of the law. One of them was a man named Oleg Borisovich Utkin and he had become a very rich man as a result. He was currently a leading figure in the Russian black market.

None of this would matter, except that our mother, while young, had dated Oleg Borisovich Utkin. She had even used her feminine charms to get information out of him that she gave to the CIA. Then she had ditched him and come to the US and lived happily ever after, sort of.

He held a grudge. He was the one who had hired Anthony to kill me twenty years earlier. When Anthony failed to uphold the contract, he had hired others to come after me. Anthony had put together a ragtag group of mercenaries to protect me. Sometime during the conflict, Anthony and two others had flown to Russia. I didn't know what had happened, but the attempts on my life had stopped.

It was this ragtag group of mercenaries that had been the first employees of Daniels' Security.

Everyone but Anthony had retired. However, they had built my reputation up and gave me a thriving business.

Alex made a small utterance that might have been a stifled cry. Her face was pale. Her hand over her mouth. I wasn't the only one that had been noticed by Oleg Borisovich over the years.

I grabbed my phone and dialed Devlin. He ignored my call. I called Anthony. He ignored my call. I called Vasilii. He also ignored my call. Finally, I called Kenzie.

"Get the hell out of Spain," I told her.

"I leave in a couple of hours," Kenzie told me. "And I have eyes on Amanda Reed right now. The Spanish authorities are about to pick her up."

"Good," I stayed on the phone for a moment, thinking of what I wanted to ask or say.

"Nadine," Kenzie interrupted my thoughts. "You need to keep your head down for a few days."

"On it," I answered and hung up. We were going to have to beef up security if Oleg Borisovich somehow figured into our plan. Or if Amanda Reed was picked up and willing to flip on Italian mobsters, the Italians might blame me for it. Of course, I was willing to deal with the Italians; Oleg Borisovich was far worse and if my family was involving him in this mess, he was definitely going to blame me.

"Dinner!" My mother yelled up the stairs. I looked at Zeke. Zeke looked at me. No one was going to be able to leave my house for a few days. This included my mother and his mother. It also included Sebastian and Alex. I wondered about Ivan, Devlin, Vladik, and Liam. My brothers were all big, bad Russian/Irish men. However, they all fit the stereotype of what a Russian looked like. They were tall with dark features, broad shoulders, developed muscles and an air of menace about them. At night, I had seen people cross the street to avoid them, one of them even had a unibrow that they waxed in the middle to make two. They were scary looking, but the opponent wasn't some street thug, it was a well-organized, crime lord who also looked like a Russian.

My apprehension about the wedding, Melina and Telisa's bonding, and my hungover Great Danes seemed nonexistent. The boogeyman was about to pop his head up and re-enter my life, even if he didn't physically manifest in front of me. I didn't want dinner. I wanted my bed and an Uzi. I also wanted a team of Navy SEALS posted around my house and for all the electronic security devices to work.

"I need a minute," I told them. Liam nodded. Sebastian patted my shoulder as he walked past. Alex and Zeke stayed. "Most of my security system is shot. Oleg Borisovich has an army at his disposal, a well-armed army. How do I protect my brothers? Or Alex's father?" He currently lived in Russia.

"My father will be protected," Alex answered, digging out her phone. I knew she was calling our uncle Niko. He was currently the head of the secret police in Russia. He could put Alex's father in protective custody. My mother's mother had been a Soviet hero and the daughter of a prominent member of the Soviet cabinet. People didn't mess with her or her family while she was alive. That protected status had continued even after her death. Few people dared to mess with the family, even after the word got out that some of them were working for the US Government. The Soviet solution had basically pack their bags for them, put them on a secret plane, and ship them here.

All bets were off when dealing with a madman who had a personal vendetta. The one story I knew to be absolutely true was that Oleg Borisovich had dismembered a woman and sent her body parts to my Uncle Niko as a form of protest against Melina's new life. Of course, it was hard to tie him to the dead woman, but Niko still worked on it when he had time. He'd even sent the Russian Mob after us. It hadn't ended well for the Russian mob. Vasilii didn't play by the rules, and he wasn't the only one. Half the family were in security, investigations, and law enforcement; the other half were mercenaries with skills that went well beyond their Spetznaz training.

"I'm not going home tonight, even with Sebastian," Alex said after she hung up the phone.

"Yeah, I don't think any of us are going anywhere for a few days. When Kenzie gets back, I'll make sure she gets escorted from the airport to here. I'd say Kenzie is a target just because she's related to me and our friend."

"On a scale of one to ten, how bad is this Oleg Borisovich?" Zeke asked.

"Remember about ten years ago, there was a massacre in Belarus that killed over a hundred people?" I asked.

"Yeah, it was a major deal that was covered up fairly well. They blamed it on a bomber, but the damage was too extensive for a single bomb."

"The Russian Secret Police believe that Oleg Borisovich organized it and supplied the weapons," I told him. "My uncle, Nikolai Igorovich, is head of the secret police, the bombing was targeted at him. However, to make sure the job got done, they set off seventeen bombs. Unfortunately, they didn't get the memo that Vasilii had heard of the plan, and Niko wasn't there. The Russians attempted to work with Belarus to minimize the damage, because they didn't have enough notice to evacuate the place completely. They also can't link it back to Oleg Borisovich."

"That's not good," Zeke said. "So, Anthony and Vasilii are going to kill him and frame him for Amanda's disappearance."

"I think so," I answered. "If anyone in the world can do it, they are the two I'd put my money on. It's also possible that Oleg Borisovich will find out about it and bomb their hotel."

"How bad is Vasilii?" Zeke asked.

"Let's just say that you don't want to irritate him," Alex said. "People who piss him off have a tendency to disappear. He dabbles with the dark side and they know he feeds information to his father, Niko, but no one touches him. It was attempted, once, Vasilii killed over thirty guys in less than seven minutes. Oleg Borisovich left us alone after Anthony and Vasilii promised to not bust up his business racket. So, Oleg does fear them."

"I didn't know that," I said.

"They did a deal with the devil to get us out of harm's way. Vasilii, Anthony, Grigorii, and Daniel paid him a visit. It worked out better for Oleg to agree to their terms." Alex looked at me, then Zeke.

"At least there was good news, they caught Amanda Reed," I sighed.

Brother #3

"You were very quiet during dinner," my mother commented.

"Yeah, I have some interesting information," I told her. We were currently cleaning up the dinner mess. The others were in the living room, trying to behave as if the world were normal.

"About what?"

"Oleg Borisovich is involved in this mess," I told her. She put down the plate she was holding and looked at me. Her face was unreadable, but the corner of her eye twitched. I waited for her to say something, but she remained quiet. "Mom?" I asked after a few minutes.

"I am thinking about who I need to call," she responded quietly.

"Vasilii has already been called and Vlad is on his way here," I told her.

"If that man lays one finger on any of my children, I will cut his balls off and stick them in his nose," she said very calmly.

"You know, you and Telisa will have to stay here until we get this sorted out," I told her.

"No I do not. That man will not hold me hostage with a threat. I'd like to see him try to come after you again. I couldn't do anything about it while your father was alive, but now that he's dead, I can do whatever I want to Oleg Borisovich." My mother took in a deep breath. "Telisa, let's go to my house and leave the kids to work on this mess. We have wedding plans to attend to."

Telisa smiled and hugged Zeke. She walked over and hugged me. My mother also hugged me. They both left.

"That did not go as planned," I said after I heard their car pull out of the drive.

"Does anything ever go as planned with our mother?" Liam asked.

"Well, no, but I thought this would go a little better than it did." I looked at him. "Do you think she'd kill him?"

"Oh yeah," Liam said.

"Maybe we should have taken her passport," I thought for a moment. "And chained her to the plumbing in the spare bathroom."

Liam's phone went off. He looked at it and smiled.

"Kenzie and Vlad are both here," he stood up.

"Kenzie and Vlad are together?" I asked.

"Vlad went to Spain today," he said.

"That's like an eight hour flight."

"On a commercial airliner, you're right. On a private jet, it's a little shorter."

"Who has a private jet?" I asked.

"Vasilii," Liam answered. Of course he did.

"How did this all get planned so fast?" I asked.

"Well, when you called Vasilii, he called Vlad. Vlad called Devlin, Devlin called me, and then mom called all of us to tell us about your wedding. So, I used that as my excuse to come home. By the time you called us, Vlad already had a plan in motion."

We all went outside. Kenzie and Vlad were getting out of a rental car. Vlad was smiling, however, that didn't mean much. My brother was terribly optimistic about everything. We seemed to live in two different worlds. In mine, everything that could go wrong, did. In his, everything that could go right, did.

"Amanda Reed is in custody," Kenzie said. "And after having a long talk with Vasilii before she was arrested, she's agreed to turn state's witness on the mob. You two are free and clear, sort of."

We all went into the house. The dogs sprang to life at seeing Vladik, their hangovers seemed to be improving. I handed Vlad a bottle of Pamprin and told him to give one to each dog. It worked wonders on hangovers. He looked at me strangely, but did as I instructed. The dogs didn't even seem to notice that he was feeding each of them a pill and not a treat.

Kenzie laid out the course of events. Alex and I had moved Amanda and given her a new identity, which she had promptly ditched. She'd had six others already in her possession, all supplied by a man named Viggo Bronson. I had questions about who tortured their children with names like that, but I kept them to myself. Viggo was a Dutchman who forged papers for a lot of criminals. He could be linked to several organized crime syndicates.

Since she had stolen money from the mob, she first went to South America and ingratiated herself with a cartel. With their protection and new papers, she'd moved to Spain to help them traffic drugs in and money out of Europe. However, this had gotten her in some hot water, as the Russians controlled a good portion of the drugs and money flowing in and out of Europe.

That made me think of more questions. Particularly, I wouldn't have minded if they brought back the show Deadliest Warrior and did Russian Mob v. South American Cartel. Gangs and the Italians had nothing on Russians and cartels.

At that point, Vlad took over, explaining Oleg Borisovich had supplied information to Vasilii about Amanda Reed, just to get her out of the way. Of course, Oleg had expected Vasilii was looking to kill her, not turn her over to the authorities. Now, he was pretty sure Oleg was feeling double crossed as one of his aliases had left Russia an hour before Vlad and Kenzie had left Spain. My stomach flopped at that statement.

Anthony and Vasilii were looking for him. Vlad was pretty sure he was coming this way. Devlin agreed, because somehow, Oleg Borisovich had gotten wind that Alex and I were involved in this fiasco. Probably because Vasilii had contacted him, but turned the woman over to the police instead of killing her. The NSA was on high alert for his presence in the US, as was Homeland Security.

After they finished, it didn't take long for Zeke to start making calls. He arranged for the handymen to come over immediately and fix the front of the house as well as the security system. I sat, numb, in a chair.

Over the years, a few big, bad wolves had come my way, most of them Russian Mob. However, they didn't scare me. Not like Oleg Borisovich, who had pulled the strings of the Russian Mob to try to have me killed on several occasions.

"We need to protect Ivan," I blurted out.

"It's being taken care of," Vlad said. I was pretty sure Vlad was CIA. I was also pretty sure Devlin worked for the NSA. They would have friends in high places. "However, he's never come after us, just you and Alex. You're women and killing women is more damaging to the Russian family structure than killing men."

To some degree, this was true. Starting in the early 1900's Russian women had gotten used to not having Russian men around. There was the Russian Revolution, World War I, World War II, Soviet leaders who liked to kill people, and poverty. In this sense, the death of a Russian woman was more damaging to the family structure. However, those days were largely behind Russia, and the value of women was being reduced some. To our misfortune, Oleg Borisovich had grown up during the Soviet era, not the new Russian era.

However, the good news was that my family had never intended to kill Oleg Borisovich. The bad news was that my family had never intended to kill Oleg Borisovich. This created mixed feelings for me. If he was dead, the Russian mob would leave me alone. However, I hated to think that my family were murderers. Even Anthony was family at this point.

Oleg Borisovich

Kenzie and Alex both snored beside me. Two of my Great Danes were also in my room. They snored louder than either girl. The Pamprin had really zonked the dogs out. However, even the pain meds and the armed guards didn't help me sleep. I tossed and turned in my normally wonderful bed. The muscles in my neck and shoulders were tight from stress. I would need to see a chiropractor and a massage therapist, if I survived long enough to make the appointment.

In the distance a dog or coyote let out a long, mournful howl. Under normal conditions, one or more of my dogs would have answered. Tonight, they were too tired to hear him and too drugged to care. Maybe I shouldn't have given them a Pamprin.

My ears strained listening for other noises. A computer or radio was playing softly downstairs, no doubt helping to keep one of the sentries awake. Beyond that, there was very little noise. The furnace groaned and popped as it heated up. However, with it being winter, there weren't any insects outside to chirp and sing.

It was too quiet. I don't live in the city, I live outside of it on a two lane black top road. My nearest neighbor is about half a mile away. It is nearly impossible to see the road or the entrance to my driveway from the house. However, there were still traffic noises.

Despite the narrow highway, it was part of suburban Kansas City. My house was one of many estates in a long line along the road. The entire area had been sold off in large wooded lots to people with enough money to purchase such things. As a result, there were teenagers coming and going at all hours. There were adults coming and going at all hours and the road was traversed by through traffic, headed to and from Raytown, as long as they didn't mind taking the back way.

Tonight there was none of that. It was eerie to hear almost nothing. I climbed from bed and headed downstairs. It was still a challenge, but I was healing. Vlad sat on the couch, a TV showed the driveway entrance. His laptop played quiet music.

"Can't sleep?" He asked.

"No, it's too quiet. How many cars have gone past?" I pointed at the TV, surprised to find one working and mounted to my wall.

"None in the last hour or so."

"Where'd the TV come from?"

"Ivan brought to us."

"That's odd." I gazed at the screen. Nothing moved on it except some tree branches in time with the wind. "It is the weekend, right?"

"Ivan bringing us a TV or that it's a Saturday night?" Vlad asked.

"It's Saturday." I said.

"Yeah," Vlad answered.

"So where are all my neighbors?"

"You don't have neighbors."

"Not in the traditional sense, but I do have neighbors. Someone should be out. There isn't any snow on the ground, no ice covering the roads, the temperatures aren't even below freezing, so where are they?"

"How much traffic are we talking about?" Vlad asked.

"Enough that I moved the sensors about twenty feet back from the road, because at least once a night, someone would set them off driving too close to the shoulder. Or someone would get lost and turn around in my driveway." I had suspicions that if the police ever put up a DUI checkpoint on the road, most of my neighbors would be spending a night in jail.

I had some perimeter alarms, but they were also near the road. The back of my land butted up to conservation land. Animals had set off the side and back perimeter alarms, so I had uninstalled them some time ago.

Anubis padded down the steps. He looked terrible, even for a dog. That would teach him to binge on booze. He went to the door and sniffed it. However, they had a doggie door through the utility room, so I didn't get up to let him out. He'd remember it soon enough. I went back to staring at the TV screen, willing some traffic to drive by.

Anubis walked over to me, I reached out to pet him, but he drew back. His teeth were bared, but he wasn't growling. The hair on his neck was standing up.

"What's wrong..." Vlad started. I stopped him with a finger to my lip. A few years earlier, a mountain lion had gotten in my house through the giant doggie door. Anubis had reacted the same way to it.

"Geht's," I whispered to the dog. Anubis didn't move towards the door, instead he moved deeper into the shadows of the living room. The big dog nudged his brother. Baldur raised his head, sniffed, and bared his teeth. Something was definitely wrong. The two began to circle the living room.

"I'll go do the same," Vlad whispered as Baldur and Anubis woke up the other dogs. The Danes spoke without verbal communication. It was interesting to watch their behavior. They were all on alert for something, something I couldn't see, smell, or touch. I wondered if it was another mountain lion or perhaps, something more dangerous.

Anubis and Baldur returned to the front door. Marduk and Set went to the utility room. Loki and Enki stayed inside, drawing near to me. Within a few moments, everyone was in my living room without any lights on. Zeke went to the front door and opened it. There was a long howl and Anubis charged out the door. I heard the flap in the utility room bang as it swung wildly. Enki and Loki began to growl, stepping backwards, moving the group of us closer together.

Danes were technically hunting dogs. However, they were also known as being loyal and protective. In my Danes, we had encouraged both their hunting and protective instincts. As the two smallest Danes herded us together, I realized I still wasn't carrying a gun with me.

The growl intensified, becoming deeper, it rumbled through the body more than it did the ears, like that of a large predatory cat. Until my Danes had done it, I didn't know it was possible for a dog to make a noise that low in frequency.

There was an inhuman noise from outside. All four Great Danes came dashing in through the utility room door. They encircled us. My brothers, Zeke, Sebastian and Alex had all drawn guns. Something warm and wet brushed my leg. Anubis was bleeding. The sound must have come from him. Zeke, Sebastian and my brothers started to communicate using hand signals. Alex and I watched as they began to spread out. Without warning, my front door exploded inwards. A cold wind blew through the entrance and into the hallway that led to the kitchen and living room. Gunshots followed, I dove to the floor as the men began to return fire. Alex and Kenzie dove with me. The Danes smothered us, keeping close.

"Nadine Seanevna Daniels!" A male voice cut through the sound of gunfire. No one used my patronymic, it wasn't even on my birth certificate. My father, Sean Daniels, had tried to erase some of our Russian traditions. I had a middle name, like most Americans, even if it was strange and Russian.

The voice was unknown to me. It was thick with a Russian accent. Deep like a bear's growl. I tried to shrug at my brothers over the backs of my dogs and wasn't sure the gesture could be seen.

"Nadine Seanevna Daniels!" The voice shouted again. If I hadn't come skipping out the first time, I certainly wasn't going to do it just because he did a second time. "I have the place surrounded." I doubted that. It was hard to get to my property through the conservation land. It was heavily protected because there was a breeding population of mountain lions in it, even though the Department of Conversation swore there wasn't.

"Stop right there," Zeke said, his gun becoming steady in his hands.

"I just want to see Nadine," the voice said.

"I don't think she wants to see you," Zeke answered.

"And who are you?" The voice asked.

"Her fiancé. Who are you?"

"Oleg Borisovich and I have something of hers." I couldn't see the boogeyman that had spent a good portion of my life trying to kill me. I really wanted to. I pushed and prodded the dogs until they let me off the ground. Great Danes are heavy and determined, so it took a moment. Alex and Kenzie stood with me. Together we rounded the corner and found he had moved from the entrance way to the kitchen.

"Finally, we meet," Oleg Borisovich gestured to me with an outstretched hand. "I have waited long time for this." Another man appeared. He was much smaller than Oleg Borisovich. He was also uglier and younger. I worked hard to keep from sneering.

Melina and Telisa were dragged into the room by their arms. I frowned. My mother had gotten her chance and missed it. We'd discuss it later. I had fully expected her to rip his heart out. Russian mothers are a lot like bears.

The Great Danes were doing something near my legs. I could feel them squirming and moving. The lights were still off and I wondered if fighting bad guys in the dark was the smartest plan.

"Let's make a deal," Oleg said to me. "I'll give you your mothers, you come with me."

"I'm not going with you and Quasimodo." I told him.

"Then I kill your mothers, and then you."

"How's that been working out for you the last twenty years?" I snarked. "How about you let Melina and Telisa go, you turn around and walk out of my house, you return to Russia and I don't tell Vasilii to kill you the moment you step foot on Russian soil?" I countered.

"So brave for someone outnumbered," Oleg glared at me, daring me to look away. I didn't. I wanted to pat myself on the back, or give myself a high five, but that would have looked silly.

"Angriefen," I told the Danes. They darted from between my legs, heading for Quasimodo. The man stumbled backwards, dragging Melina and Telisa to the ground. Oleg Borisovich raised his gun, but Baldur crashed into him. The two fell against my new stove. "I hope there's a warranty." I hadn't meant to say it out loud, but sometimes my brain and mouth weren't on the same page. I would have to call Katya about any damage done to it. Maybe she'd give me a new one just so she could look at Zeke again.

Weird Behaviors, Normal Day

Baldur worried Oleg's arm until he dropped the gun. The dog let go of his arm and grabbed his thigh. Oleg's blows glanced off the Dane's head as he began to drag him towards the utility room. Then he suddenly stopped. Baldur let go of Oleg and let out a long howl that made my ears hurt. The other dogs responded. Anubis grabbed my mother by her skirt, Marduk grabbed her leg and they began pulling her towards us. Enki, Loki and Set grabbed Telisa, who was actually smaller than my own mother by a few inches and a few pounds. They also moved towards us.

Quasimodo was rolling around on the floor, holding different parts of his body and whimpering. I grabbed a cell phone and began to dial 911.

"911, please state your emergency."

"This is Nadine Daniels, there is a Russian crime lord in my house," I responded.

"Miss Daniels, I am dispatching police now. Do you know the man that broke into your house?"

"Oleg Borisovich Utkin," I told her. "There's something wrong with my Great Danes, please alert officers of their presence."

"Miss Daniels, my supervisor is recommending you exit the house if at all possible. Oleg Borisovich Utkin is wanted by several agencies in both the US and Europe." The operator told me.

"Yes, I am aware. He's been trying to kill me for roughly twenty years because my mom broke up with him before I was born. I also have a secret service agent and another government agent at my house, but they're my brothers." I told her. Sometimes I was overly informative.

"It appears that Officer Diego Vasquez has requested to speak with you directly, may I connect him?" The operator asked.

"Sure," I said.

"What on earth are you doing with a Russian king pin in your house?" Diego wasn't shouting but I wouldn't have been surprised if he had been.

"Having a bad day."

"I have no replies to that. I'm on my way, it will be like three minutes," Diego said.

"Make it two and I'll give you a cookie," I told him and hung up, forgetting that I was on the phone with 911. Alex and Sebastian were untying Melina and Telisa. Zeke and Vlad were tying up Oleg Borisovich. Liam was dealing with Quasimodo. My dogs were jumping around and barking, poking at the backdoor. I finally opened it just to get them out of the way and hoped they didn't get shot by the arriving officers.

Then the Danes began running back and forth. Anubis, still bleeding, grabbed onto me and jerked my pajama bottoms, ripping them down one side. I struggled to keep them on as I scolded him. Enki joined the fun and began tugging on Alex. Baldur grabbed Melina, who was still on the floor and began dragging her outside. My mother, determined to keep her skirt down, didn't fight the dog off.

"That's odd," I said.

"Let's see what they want," Telisa stood up and followed my mother and Enki outside. Alex, Kenzie, and I exchanged looks. They were armed, so we followed the mothers.

The air outside was cold. Once we were outside, barefoot on the cold ground, three of the dogs darted back inside. Anubis growled when I stepped towards the house. Enki and Set kept tugging Melina closer to the woods. There were strobing lights in the distance. I was pretty sure I owed Diego Vasquez a cookie. I followed Enki, scolding him and trying to convince him to release my mother. She was going to be really unhappy when she got loose. I felt sorry for the Danes, particularly Enki.

From the house there was shouting. Baldur had Zeke by the pajamas, Zeke was struggling to walk and keep his pants from coming down. Loki and Marduk were herding Liam outside. Vlad and Sebastian were both following, shouting at the dogs. I had no clue what their deal was.

The police cruiser turned down my driveway. I motioned to it, to let Vasquez know that I was not in the house. He got out of his cruiser and walked towards us.

"Where's Oleg Utkin?" Vasquez asked.

"Tied up in my house," I told him. He took a step and Anubis growled at him. "What's wrong with your dog?"

"I don't know," I answered. "He's been injured, but that doesn't usually make him aggressive. His brothers are all acting that same strange way."

Another patrol car started down my drive. I watched the lights for a second and was suddenly swept from my feet. Everything hurt as I stared up at the sky. Little bits of stuff wafted through the air around me.

"Did my house just blow up?" I asked.

"Yes," Vasquez answered. He was lying next to me on the ground. "I think I know why your dogs were being aggressive."

"Not the entire house," Zeke said. "It looks like it was mainly the kitchen, utility room, and the spare bedroom."

"Oh." That didn't make it any better. I sat up. Smoke was pouring through the hole in the side of my house. Flames licked at the remnants of construction materials.

"Why did my house blow up?" I asked. "Was Oleg Borisovich inside? Did he plant a bomb?"

"Yes, he was still inside," Sebastian answered.

"No, I think it was your stove," Liam said. "Dmitri and Pytor are great at moving heavy appliances, but they suck at hooking them up."

"Oh." Tears started to run down my face.

"We'll have the fire department look for survivors and bodies," Vasquez patted me on the shoulder and stood up. The tears flowed harder.

"Please don't cry," Zeke grabbed hold of me, pulling me into him. "We'll rebuild the kitchen and utility room and spare room. We'll rebuild and make it bigger and better. I'll rebuild you an entire house if you just stop crying."

"Promise?" I wept.

"Yes."

"Ah, that's so beautiful," Kenzie cooed.

"This marriage is going to be wonderful," Melina said.

"They are perfect," Telisa agreed. I cried even harder, but it was hidden by Zeke's shoulder.

Wedding Plans

They found both Quasimodo and Oleg Borisovich alive inside my house. The fight between Oleg and Baldur had knocked the gas line loose on my stove. As the two Russians attempted to flee the house, something had sparked, setting off the explosion. It had thrown them clear, but between the dog damage and the explosion damage, they were in no condition to make a run for it.

Zeke had kept his promise and my house was under construction, by real contractors. He was even expanding it. My mother had tried to get us to stay with her while the repairs were being done, but we had checked into a hotel, two rooms despite the fact that we were still getting married. The days were ticking away rather quickly.

Amanda Reed and Fred Reed spilled their guts on everyone they had ever been involved with. It was making the justice department very happy.

They'd both been granted immunity for their testimony. It made me feel ill.

Or maybe it was wedding jitters.

Hadena James

I've been writing for over two decades and before that, I was creating my own bedtime stories to tell myself. I penned my first short story at the ripe old age of 8. It was a fable about how the raccoon got its eye-mask and was roughly three pages of handwritten, 8 year old scrawl. My mother still has it and occasionally, I still dig it out and admire it.

When I got my first computer, I took all my handwritten stories and typed them in. Afterwards, I tossed the originals. In my early twenties, I had a bit of a writer's meltdown and deleted everything. So, with the exception of the story about the raccoon, I actually have none of my writings from before I was 23. Which is sad, because I had a half dozen other novels and well over two hundred short stories. It has all been offered up to the computer and writing gods as a sacrifice and show of humility or some such nonsense that makes me feel less like an idiot about it.

I have been offered contracts with publishing houses in the past and always turned them down. Now that I have experimented with being an Indie Author, I really like it and I'm really glad I turned them down. However, if you had asked me this in the early years of 2000, I would have told you that I was an idiot (and it was a huge contributing factor to my deleting all my work).

When I'm not writing, I play in a steel-tip dart league and enjoy going to dart tournaments. I enjoy renaissance festivals and sanitized pirates who sing sea shanties. My appetite for reading is ferocious and I consume two to three books a week as well as writing my own. Aside from introducing me to darts, my SO has introduced me to camping, which I, surprisingly, enjoy. We can often be found in the summer at Mark Twain Lake in Missouri, where his parents own a campground.

I am a native of Columbia, Missouri, which I will probably call home for the rest of my life, but I love to travel. Day trips, week trips, vacations on other continents, wherever the path takes me is where I want to be and I'm hoping to be able to travel more in the future.

http://www.facebook.com/hadenajames
hadenajames.wordpress.com
@hadenajames

Made in the USA
Monee, IL
31 August 2024

65003226R00095